SURRENDER, AT LAST . . .

"Come here, little bit." Two arms wrapped about her, hauling her down beside him. A heavy thigh clamped over her legs, locking them immobile.

Shackled by the strength of his body, her head tucked beneath his chin, Sami squirmed but could not dislodge his hold. "Mr. Woden!"

"I've watched that pretty little mouth talk and wondered how your lips would taste, half-pint," he murmured. "I bet they're as sweet as high-meadow flowers." A callused hand cupped her jaw, tilting her face toward his lips.

"Mmmm." Sami's protest slid back into her throat, muffled by the pressure of his lips.

A heartbeat later, he murmured against her mouth, "Easy now, little bit. Easy. I won't hurt you."

His mouth teased hers. Tantalizing kisses prowled the soft contours of her lips. As his mouth played tenderly on hers, Sami felt her taut body yield to the mellow warmth, easing her curves to fit the hard lines of his body . . .

Diamond Books by Cait Logan

TAME THE FURY
RUGGED GLORY

RUGGED GLORY

CAIT LOGAN

DIAMOND BOOKS, NEW YORK

RUGGED GLORY

A Diamond Book / published by arrangement with
the author

PRINTING HISTORY
Second Chance at Love edition published 1986
Diamond edition / September 1991

ISBN: 1-55773-582-4

Diamond Books are published by The Berkley Publishing Group,
200 Madison Avenue, New York, New York 10016.
The name "DIAMOND" and its logo are trademarks
belonging to Charter Communications, Inc.

PRINTED IN THE UNITED STATES OF AMERICA

10 9 8 7 6 5 4 3 2 1

For my three *dearling* daughters —
Kerry, Karla, and Lana.
And for my sister, my friend — Donna.

- 1 -

"HEY, YOU GUYS, that's enough! If one more person shoots me, I won't care if this *is* the last day of school, I'll keep the entire class for an additional hour," Sami Lassiter threatened. The water streams from the few remaining squirt guns stopped, and Sami lowered the drenched notebook that had served as her shield against the impromptu attack.

Warily, she placed the notebook on her desk and sat in the chair behind it. She took off her glasses and dried them with a tissue. On the wall behind her, the clock's hands moved toward dismissal time. As though following the movements of a yo-yo, the third graders alternately raised their eyes to the clock, then lowered them to their teacher.

At exactly five minutes before three o'clock, Sami checked her wristwatch. She patted the thick ebony-colored coil on top of her head with a dry tissue, then replaced her glasses.

"We have a few remaining moments, class." She

smiled and pointed to the array of water pistols on her desk. "You may collect your weapons from the principal's confiscation drawer next fall. They'll have your names on them."

Sami paused, then said, "I hope you enjoy your summer vacation to the hilt. You may leave now."

When the last moist farewell kiss had dried up on her cheek and the last student had gone, Sami began to realize how exhausted she was. She normally taught high school students, and maintaining control of the third grade class throughout the harrowing day had been a challenge. She leaned back in the chair and slowly rubbed the tight cords at the back of her neck. "The last day of school and the natives showed the substitute teacher no mercy," she murmured.

She stared at the serenity of the Rocky Mountains, snow-capped and covered with spruce and pine, beyond the classroom window. The Wyoming mountains were majestic, and Sami felt they ought to stir her senses, but just now she felt drained of emotion.

Her husband would have loved to paint the scenery around Lone Pine. But a car wreck had ended Des's life three years ago. Sami sighed as she remembered a more recent but equally devastating blow—the death of her sister, Ann, six months ago. The legal battle in Arkansas to win custody of her nieces from their abusive and neglectful father had cost Sami the last of her savings. Her lawyer had been good—but to pay his fees she had had to accept this makeshift position as a substitute elementary teacher at the Lone Pine School. She did not have the luxury of waiting for another job more appropriate to her training and experience.

Earlier in the year, Sami had been busy with legalities and the adjustments of her new family. She had not been able to apply and interview for fall teaching positions and hoped there'd be a high school vacancy still open as she began job hunting this summer. "I *have* to start sending out application letters—tomorrow," she promised herself aloud.

Her trigger finger slid into place on a pink Colt .45, filled with water clear up to its rubber plug. Closing one eye, Sami sighted down the plastic barrel and aimed it at the parking lot just beyond her window. She idly squeezed the trigger to vent her frustration. "Bam."

The mountain shadows had begun to creep over the pavement. White-bark pines bordered the parking lot, filtering the midafternoon Wyoming sun. A mud-spattered four-wheeler slid into the slot next to Sami's battered red Volkswagen. The outline of a straw hat brim and the broad shoulders of a tall man filled the shadowy cab.

Sami straightened her petite frame and sighted down the Colt barrel at the man: "Bam. That's just fer being out yonder while I've still got to scrub blackboards," she drawled.

For a moment, the man's large hand rested on the rearview mirror. The door opened, and a western boot heel hit the concrete, followed by a long leg sheathed in faded blue denim.

The man stood free of the late-model Bronco and closed the mud-splattered door. With his right hand he lifted his worn straw hat; then his left hand sifted through his dark hair. Its thickness softened his broad brow and curled over the collar of his shirt.

In the sunlight, his hard-boned face was the shade of burnished leather. His black brows glistened in the sun, shadowing deep-set eyes. His nose was slightly crooked, as if it had once been broken, and his high cheekbones stood out above an uncompromising jaw-line.

Sami narrowed her eyes, focusing on the man's face. It was strong, elemental—the kind to make women pay attention, as she was doing now. She half smiled, admitting to a certain stirring of her feminine senses even as her soul and mind recoiled.

Sami pumped the plastic trigger of the squirt gun lightly as the man turned toward her classroom window. Dressed in dusty work clothes, he exuded a raw masculinity that would cause any woman's heart to flutter—any woman's except Sami's. His shoulders lifted and the faded pink western shirt stretched tightly against his broad chest. He looked as much a part of the Rockies as the buttes or the aspen leaves trembling on the late May breeze. He replaced the hat and strode toward the school entrance. Flat-bellied and lean-hipped, he moved with a hunter's long-legged stalk.

"Bam. That's because you look like my father, cowboy. 'Bout the same size and you move like him." With the barrel of the squirt gun, she followed him across the lot. "A lot younger of course, and without the beer belly, but you look to be just as mean and shiftless." Opening her eyelids slightly, Sami watched the man's lithe walk. "How old *are* you, cowboy? Between thirty and fifty, I reckon."

She swallowed the dry wadding that filled her throat each time she saw a big man move with that confident grace. The man beyond the window bore the same "good ole boy" aura as her father, twanging of taverns and brawls. She shuddered, forcing her thoughts away from the past. Arkansas was a lifetime away, she reminded herself.

Minutes later, Ray Medford, the high school principal, stood in the open doorway of her classroom. "Ms. Lassiter, you have a visitor."

He opened the door wider, and Sami saw the virile stranger standing beside him. Next to the well-groomed, business-suited principal, the cowboy resembled a character from a Zane Grey book. His left hand loosely held the battered straw hat; his rumpled sable hair was flecked with gray.

Feeling guilty about her playful shooting of the stranger, Sami gave the principal a cordial smile. "Please come in, Mr. Medford," she invited him as she straightened the record books on her desk, then methodically arranged the squirt guns in a line on top of them. She hoped the man hadn't seen her aim at him, and to calm herself, she took a deep breath and counted slowly. One . . . two . . . three . . .

At close range, she guessed the stranger to be around forty. He was rawboned, lean. Toughened like the boots he wore. The tiny lines scoring his dark skin indicated that he spent much of his time outdoors. Lighter creases appeared at the corners of his black-lashed lids. Over the slightly crooked nose, raven brows, drawn into a single heavy line by his frown, shadowed intense gray eyes.

Deeply set in the rugged face, his eyes pierced her own, then rose to the sleek coil of hair anchored on top of her head. His gaze rested there a moment, then slid over the tinted lenses of her glasses to the bow-shaped curve of her upper lip. The smoky gray eyes stared at the fullness of her bottom lip as though gauging her sensuality. A hot, dry wind seemed to sweep over Sami's flesh as the probing stare reached the dimple in the center of her chin.

Her breasts tingled within her sensible cotton bra as the cowboy explored the fullness covered by her white eyelet blouse. Uncomfortable beneath his steady examination, Sami pressed her palms down on the oak desktop, her fingers splayed over the stack of record books. She pushed her lips into a smile. "Mr. Medford?"

"Ah . . . yes, Ms. Lassiter. This is Ben Woden. Ben, meet Samantha Lassiter."

The big man moved directly in front of her desk to study her. The steel-gray eyes raked her once more. They darkened within the frames of black lashes. His head dipped toward her. "Ma'am."

The single word expressed displeasure. It rumbled up the brown, corded neck and slid grimly through his slightly parted lips. The left corner of his mouth lifted and fell quickly; then the hard lips pressed tightly together.

The muscular legs locked into an arrogant stance, boots spread apart on the tile floor. One thumb hooked into the tooled leather belt riding his hips. The strong, blunt-tipped fingers of his other hand tightened about the curved brim of the hat, rolling it.

"Samantha?" Ray prompted. "Aren't you feeling well?"

Sami glanced at the principal, then back to the man standing before her. Ben Woden was rough. Elemental. A cowboy from his boots to his sable hair. He was lean and muscular, and Sami sensed that a woman locked within his arms would be sensually satisfied.

Her body tightened against the shudder she could feel moving through her bones and raising goose bumps on her flesh. All her adult life, she had avoided men of his type. Now this cowboy's rawly masculine components jarred every tightly controlled muscle in her body. She felt like a cat with raised hackles.

"How do you do, Mr. Woden?" She pushed the words from her brain onto her tongue and through her lips.

"I do fine, ma'am," he drawled. "But you just went white. Is something wrong?"

The low, sensual rasp of his voice brought Sami's hand fluttering protectively to her suddenly dry throat. The pulse there beat a wild tattoo against her palm. "I . . . I'm fine. Just a little harried. The children had last-day-of-school nerves." In explanation, she motioned toward the plastic guns on her desk.

Ray laughed. "Then it was true. Bobby Wilson said you were the class's target for their last squirt-gun war."

Sami didn't understand the gleam in the cowboy's eyes. She moved to the edge of the chair, the tips of her toes just touching the floor. Somehow he'd made her feel like an auctioned-off heifer who did not quite justify the buyer's bid. "Their 'war' lasted all of one whole minute," she said defensively.

"Now, Samantha. The last day of school is hard for everyone." Ray glanced uneasily at the cowboy's deepening frown. "Mr. Woden has backed the school for years, Samantha. His donations range from jungle gyms for the playground to textbooks to gym floors. He also provides a hefty scholarship each year for a graduating senior and—"

"There's no need to go into all that, Ray. Either she's qualified and she's going to do the job or she's not," Woden interrupted. His left hand, which had been hooked into his belt, rose to rub the unrelenting contour of his jaw slowly. The sound of stubble against callused skin raised the fine hairs on the nape of Sami's neck. "And if a bunch of little third graders can get the better of her for all of one whole minute,"—he repeated her words—"how the hell is she going to manage my boy?"

He paused to flick a downward glance at Sami. "She's cute as a bug's ear. But look at her, she's half grown and looks about as seasoned as one of my heifers." He compressed his hard mouth, the line between his brows deepening with dissatisfaction.

Sami repeated his words inside her head. Bug's ear? Half grown? Heifer? She was thirty-two years old, held a master's degree in special education, and was raising two children by herself. She'd had to claw her way out of ignorance and poverty, and she had worked sixteen hour days to do it.

She'd seen a man she deeply cared for slip gallantly from life. She had taught at high schools for over ten years before fate and the broken-down red bug had landed her in Lone Pine. The small town was no more than a wide spot on U.S. Highway 287 and 26, just north of Dubois.

The cowboy standing before her was typical of the one-grocery-store, five-taverns-town breed.

"I've missed something here, Ray." Sami spoke

softly. "Why is Mr. Woden concerned with my size and appearance?" None of the rancher's objections had anything to do with her ability to teach. At first sight, she had intuitively disliked this man; now she *knew* she did not like him. Not only was his demeanor abrasive, but his size intimidated her. Ray was a six-footer, and Ben Woden towered over him by a good four inches.

"Maybe we should all sit down and discuss the matter." Ray glanced at the rows of desks, gauging their small size. "Ben and I aren't going to fit into these desks."

"Hell, man, I don't have time for a long-winded discussion. Matt Dobson's watching the bull I just bought at the auction. The Baron is two thousand pounds of prime seed bull. He could crush Dobson's holding pen as easy as toothpicks. He's got to be at my ranch before dark."

His eyes pierced Sami's. "Look, ma'am. My boy, Mike, has problems. He's almost seventeen and as cantankerous as the Baron."

He swallowed, causing the cords in his neck to stand out in taut relief. He glanced beyond the windows, seeming to focus on the mountains' rugged magnificence. The deep, raspy voice faltered. "He's got problems I don't know how to deal with. Mixes with the wrong crowd for one."

He shifted his weight from his left foot to his right as he turned to her. "He didn't graduate from high school. Dropped out last year." His hand swept finger-trails through his thick dark hair. "Hell, maybe he takes after me; I dropped out, too. But I've been talking to Ray, and he says there's a thing now called the GED that would be the same as a high school diploma. He told me that you might be available to help Mike get ready for the GED exam."

Sami nodded to indicate her interest.

"I pay good, ma'am, I'll triple anything the school pays, plus room and board for you and your girls." Ben

Woden continued earnestly, "We have a housekeeper, Emma, so don't think you'd be hired to do dishes. You'd live with us, tutor my boy, and tend your nieces. If you do your job well, I'll add a hefty bonus to your check at the end of the summer. Meanwhile, you'll have whatever you need. I'll see to it."

He tilted his head sideways. "But if you don't do the job, you're out on your fanny. What do you say, ma'am?"

Ray cleared his throat. "Ah, Ben, Ms. Lassiter. . ." he began.

Sami frowned. The cowboy was flat-out blunt-spoken and she didn't like him. She weighed that against the fact that her June rent was due in two days, and her bank balance resembled a pancake with a hole in it. Moreover, she needed art supplies to begin painting the landscapes she hoped to sell to tourists. The more her thoughts dwelt on her financial situation, the more the monetary incentive to take the job overshadowed her antagonism toward Ben Woden.

"I can speak for myself, Ray." She tried to smile up at the man's fierce frown. "Mr. Woden, I'll have to think it over, of course. But the idea sounds intriguing and I *am* interested."

His frown deepened; his long legs locked into a rigid stance. "Interested? Intriguing? Those are polite words, but they don't tell me what I want to know. I need your answer right now, yes or no. Woman, my boy is twice your size and tough as an old boot. I'd say no teacher could handle him, much less a half-pint prima donna with starch in her panties."

"Ben . . ." Ray's tone cautioned.

Sami felt the blood heat up in the tips of her toes and warm her red leather pumps. Anger seemed to surge through her veins. Her palms began to tingle, and she braced them on the desktop as she stood. She felt her face flush, felt the rising heat throb against the pearl studs in her earlobes.

"I am qualified by the Wyoming Department of Education to teach teenagers with learning problems, Mr. Woden." She added, "You may check my credentials, which are on file in Ray's office." She trembled with anger, an emotion she had never allowed herself to express. In an effort to soothe her temper, she took a deep breath, licked the dryness from her lips, and exhaled. "My height and the starch in my panties are not relevant to the position you've offered me. Your manners, however, are."

Woden's thick eyebrows lifted with surprise. "What's wrong with them?"

"They're atrocious," Sami stated flatly. "I have two young girls, Mr. Woden. I am reluctant to expose them to a . . . rough element just now." Several loose school papers crumpled beneath her hands. Sami heard the sound and straightened, lacing her fingers across her stomach to stop them from trembling. She craned her neck to stare back at the cowboy.

The big hand went to his jaw and rubbed the stubble there. His eyes narrowed slowly, and a smile played at the corners of his mouth, softening the curve of his lower lips. The slight movement grew into a white-toothed smile suitable for a billboard. He glanced at Ray. "Peppery, isn't she?"

Ray's chuckle died when he looked at Sami. "Ms. Lassiter is a believer in courtesy, Ben. But's she tough, too. And, as she said, she's qualified. I'd have her on board here permanently if there were a vacancy on the high school staff."

Sami's palms sweated against each other. She badly needed this Wyoming grubstake. "I can handle the job, Mr. Woden. But *you* are to handle your manners. Is that agreed?"

"I'll work on it, lady." The Wyoming drawl caused a feathery sensation to travel down her spine. Sami's eyes narrowed at the tone. A lady-killer on the prowl. But the lady wasn't interested.

"You do that."

"I thought we could work something out . . ." the principal began.

The cowboy fitted the battered hat over his dark brown hair and adjusted the angle of it until the rolled brim shadowed his eyes. "How soon can you start?"

"Right away. I'll need an advance on my salary and directions to your ranch," Sami said crisply. She hadn't liked the hungry male gleam in Ben Woden's smoky gray eyes. Not a bit.

"Do you need help moving? What are you driving?" he asked in rapid-fire succession.

Sami answered the second question by pointing toward her red Volkswagen in the parking lot. "My car is next to yours."

He glanced at the car, then looked back at her. "Cute, but it wouldn't make the road to my ranch. Store it someplace for the summer, and I'll move you."

Sami met his challenging stare with one of her own. Much as she disliked agreeing with Woden over any matter, at the moment her car was not fit transportation on any road. "I'd appreciate that very much."

He nodded, then withdrew a worn leather checkbook from his hip pocket. He opened it, placed it on her desk, and took out a pen. Bracing his hands against the desk, he stared at her. "When shall I pick you up?"

The June rent was due the day after tomorrow, Sami reminded herself quickly. She had to pay it or move. "Tomorrow afternoon will be suitable."

"Suitable!" he snorted. "Another polite word. You look like you know a lot of them, lady." The big tanned hand scrawled a generous figure on the check and signed it in bold slashes. Woden ripped it out, straightened, and handed it to her. "Shake?"

The palm stretched out to her was callused and double the size of her own. Sami swallowed and extended her hand. Instantly, he encased the softness of hers, warming it. She jerked her hand free and, behind her back, wiped his touch from her palm.

The steel-colored eyes darkened. Woden's big body rippled before it went rigid. "Agreed. Be ready tomorrow afternoon. I know where you live."

Sami collapsed in her chair after Ray and Woden left. From his sable-colored hair to his leather work boots, Ben Woden was an upsetting man. Automatically, she contrasted the cowboy's abrupt manner to Des's soft-spoken kindness. She missed Des's companionable warmth, the challenge of their intellectual debates over a fine dinner. She missed Des.

Eileen O'Rourke stacked another cardboard box on the mound in the corner of the trailer living room. "You're kidding! Ben Woden?"

Sami carefully wedged a bundle of long-handled art brushes inside a box of paint tubes on the kitchen counter. She shrugged her ponytail back over her shoulder and pulled down her TEACHERS NEED LOVE, TOO T-shirt. "You know him?"

Eileen plopped onto the battered couch and spread her long legs before her. "Ben Woden," she repeated, laying her hand over her heart.

Sami laughed, padded barefoot to her friend, and asked, "Well, are you done swooning?"

"Just barely. I heard he asked about you last week." Eileen's lids drooped to half-mast. "Turn around."

"You're crazy. But I'll humor you." Sami pivoted and grinned down at Eileen's contemplative expression. "What's going on in that criminal brain of yours?"

"Even in a T-shirt and worn jeans with your hair pulled back into a ponytail, and no makeup, you're a beauty, kid. I'd say you could give Ben Woden a race for his money. The bigger they are, the harder they fall." Eileen grinned. "Shoot, I bet your soft little Arkie drawl knocked him flat." She motioned to the other end of the couch. "Have a seat, dear. Mama wants to talk."

"Eileen, you know the kids are just over at Rhonda's for a half-hour or so. I have to get all the packing done so we can go to bed early." But Sami sat and propped her feet on the coffee table. "I am tired. I've been going nonstop since school let out." She counted off on her fingers all the errands she'd run. "First to the bank to deposit his check. I've never had a two-thousand dollar check written to my name before."

"Neither have I," Eileen said dryly. "Go on."

"Then I picked up some art supplies and took the girls to the dry goods store. I got them sneakers with Velcro snaps, and the sound of them being ripped open every two minutes is maddening. Let's see, they got clothing, Smurf stuff, granola bars, vitamins . . ."

Sami lifted her eyes to her friend's and sighed. "It seems good to have some money, for a change. Do you know that my sister's grave doesn't even have a proper marker, and I couldn't afford to buy one? I just had to get those children away from there."

Eileen patted Sami's knees. "And by gum, you did it, kiddo. I can see a lot of changes in them already . . . they're starting to trust people."

"You think so?" Sami brightened momentarily, then sighed. "It's rough raising kids alone."

"Now, honey," Eileen continued, "I know you miss your husband at times like this, but you and the kids are headed for a new life. By the way, have you told the girls about the move?"

"Yes. I barely mentioned horses and calves, and they climbed the walls. This is going to be just what they need, Eileen. If everything works out, it'll give me the chance to tutor them on the side and bring them up to grade level."

"Of course it will." Eileen's tone closed the door on doubt about that at least. "You're not having second thoughts?"

"Just about the fact that the man paying the tab reminds me of someone I'd rather forget. He's got the same walk, the same gleam in his eye."

"Don't go into this job carrying a prejudice like that, Sami. Keep in mind that Ben Woden is highly thought of in these parts. Actually, his background is pretty colorful. His dad had a fit when Ben joined the rodeo circuit years ago and married an Indian bareback rider. Then, much later, the old man called Ben home—needed him to work the ranch."

"Was the bareback rider Mike's mother?" Sami asked.

"Uh-huh. The old man died of drinking. Two years later, Ben's wife was killed in a car wreck."

Eileen watched Sami draw circles with one fingertip. "You're doing the right thing, Sami. You and the kids need this summer. And Ben's a good guy." She shrugged. "He does raise a little hell at the Wagon Wheel once in a while. But he doesn't hurt anyone, and he always pays for the damage. And he does what he can for people." She paused, then continued, "Honey, he's the most eligible bachelor in the state. He runs a few cattle on his ranch for sentimental reasons, and he manages Woden and Son Multicorporation from his home. Not only does he own condominiums and office buildings in Casper, but he's president of Woden Lumber, Woden Mineral Enterprises, and more. If he's not already a multimillionaire, he'll be one someday, and you've got the equipment to make his poor lonely heart spin."

"Eileen! I have no romantic interest in the man. He's hired me to do a job, and I'm going to do it. It's nothing but a business arrangement, okay?"

"Mm-hm."

"I don't like your tone, Eileen. Go home and stop matchmaking."

Eileen rose to her full six feet and sauntered to the door. She opened it and stepped into the night air.

"Don't worry about your VW. It'll be okay in my garage. As for you and Ben Woden, I'm taking bets starting now."

"Auntie! Come kiss us good night," six-year-old Mary Jane demanded from the bed she shared with seven-year-old Lori. "We want to hear about the ranch again."

Lori's voice joined her sister's. "And about the cows and the damn horses."

Sami lifted her hair through the neck opening of her man-sized T-shirt. The heavy black tresses spilled down her back. "Don't curse, Lori," she called from her room. "Remember, we talked about nice words and bad words?"

Silence indicated that the girls were recalling the discussion. Sami shook her head, then glanced at her reflection in the full-length mirror on the wall. In the dimly lit room, shadows crossed her oval face. The curtain formed by her hip-length hair separated, framing the uptilted tips of her breasts. The shirt concealed her modest cotton panties and ended at midthigh. Proportionately long, her legs were slender, yet femininely curved. Sami wiggled her feet against the carpeting and stood on tiptoe.

Ben Woden's image seemed to slide over her own in the mirror, and a chill moved over her. Big men, especially arrogant or swaggering ones, always brought the same reaction.

"Auntie! Are you coming?"

Sami slid back into reality. "You betcha. Move over, here I come."

She turned off the hallway lights and stepped into her nieces' bedroom. In the shadows, the girls' heads turned toward her. "Get between us, Auntie, so's we can each have a shoulder pillow."

"I want to hear more about the d—the horses," Lori demanded after Sami settled between them.

"Honey, I wish I knew more about Mr. Woden's ranch," Sami said. "We're just going to have to wait until tomorrow. Then Mr. Woden himself is going to drive us there."

Mary Jane tugged a strand of Sami's hair and rubbed it against her face as Lori slid her thin leg over Sami's, her instep prowling her aunt's shin. "Where is Mr. Woden's ranch?"

Sami smoothed the black hair resting on her shoulder. "Eileen says it's out beyond Lost Miner's Pass."

"What about the man, Auntie?" Lori asked sleepily.

"He's well thought of in the area, honey."

"What does he look like, Auntie?" Mary Jane chimed in.

"He's a big man," Sami replied. A big man with smoky gray eyes that challenged her, she thought before drifting off to sleep. But challenged her to what?

- 2 -

SHE WAS AWAKENED sometime later by a loud pounding. Wedged between the two small girls, Sami shifted uncomfortably. She lifted Mary Jane's knee and eased the girl to her own side of the bed. Lori's hand flopped open on Sami's cheek just as the pounding was repeated, thumping the metal trailer door twice more.

Sami lifted Lori's hand from her face, turning to her left side. She pulled free a strand of her own hair from beneath the girl's dark curls and looked at the bedside clock. The hands read three o'clock.

The thump became the sound of a battering ram.

Cautiously, Sami slid from the tangle of arms and legs and worked her way through the darkness to the hallway light switch.

The pounding began again, threatening to loosen the door's hinges. It stopped when she clicked on the light. Sami raced to her own room, grabbed Des's flannel robe, and shoved her arms through the sleeves.

"Just a minute," she called. She turned on the living

room lamp, drew the curtain aside, and peered at the front steps.

Bam! The next blow rattled the door's hinges.

Sami hurriedly padded toward the door. "This better be good," she muttered as she unlocked the door and cautiously turned the knob.

Ben Woden's fist knocked the door open. Outlined in the doorway, he looked even taller than he had the day before. Maybe it was the jaunty angle of the buckskin Stetson he wore. He touched the brim in a casual greeting. "Ma'am."

Woden's boots shifted on the welcome mat as though it had rolled beneath him. He braced his hands on either side of the doorway. His breath wafted toward Sami's nostrils.

"You've been drinking, Mr. Woden." She drew Des's robe about her and tied the cloth belt. "You'd better go home."

"Can't." His fingers tightened on the door frame. He looked as though he were afraid the concrete porch would depart for China. "Got to talk to you, ma'am."

"Tomorrow, Mr. Woden." Sami inched her body behind the door and began to close it.

Woden pushed it open. "Deal's off. You can keep the money." He gazed down at her face. The thick-lashed lids closed and slowly opened. "Did you shrink?" he asked slowly, distinctly.

Sami counted to ten. She did not intend to indulge the drunken giant on her doorstep. "We will talk about this tomorrow, Mr. Woden. When you're in a more rational state. Good night."

"You're not going to close this door in my face, ma'am." Through the shadows, Sami saw his grin. It was not nice.

Mentally, she counted the steps to the telephone, then dismissed the idea. She lifted her head. She'd handled drunks, mean ones, at a very young age.

"What do you mean, 'deal's off'? Have you changed

your mind?" Woden's offer was the perfect solution to her financial dilemma.

With his palm, he rubbed the stubble-covered jaw. "Mike didn't like the idea." His low growl revealed frustration. "He pitched a fit like some loco bull." Woden's big hand swept downward, inches from Sami's body. "Hell, look at you. Mike could really hurt you if he threw a book at you, like he did me."

Before she could respond, he leaned into the room, towering over Sami, and squinted down at her. "I thought you were taller." He ducked his head and followed his boots into the small room, brushing Sami aside.

"You've got a nerve . . ." Sami was already nettled by being awakened at three o'clock. Her composure slipped fractionally; she could feel it ooze out her bare toes. She did not like the feeling of losing control—or the man who had caused it.

"I don't care who you are, Ben Woden," she snapped. "Rancher, businessman, or benefactor to thousands. You are not waltzing into my home for a friendly pre-dawn conversation, nor will I let you cancel my summer job." She bit her bottom lip and glared at him.

The large man studied the worn bareness of the room. He tipped the buckskin hat to the back of his head, revealing tousled, dark brown hair. It curled down over his broad forehead. A brown leather jacket clung to his massive shoulders. Beneath it, a sand-colored dress shirt framed the width of a tanned neck. The top three pearl snap buttons were open. Gray and black hair sprang from the V of the shirt, covering a chest that had to be the color of dark leather.

Noting his tight-fitting cream-colored Levi's, Sami fought the involuntary slide of her stare downward by examining the huge bronze belt buckle. The word "Champion" above the imprinted image of a bucking horse and rider shone in the lamplight.

Woden shifted his weight to one foot, and the play of muscles in his thighs drew her eyes lower. The knife-sharp crease of his jeans flattened across his upper legs, then fell a long distance to the arch of his polished dress boots.

He braced both hands on the counter separating the living room from the kitchen. A deep indrawn breath expanded his chest, held, then escaped in a tired sigh. "I won't hurt you, ma'am."

Sami wrapped her arms about her chest, fingers gripping her forearms. She shivered. Was it the cold night air from the open door? Or was it the rumbling pain of the tall rancher?

The dim light touched the rugged contours of his face. Deep lines were etched in the dark skin, shadows circling his eyes. His big hands tightened on the Formica countertop, and his boots spread wider.

His slow whiskey drawl fluttered over Sami. "Don't be frightened. I'll leave in a minute."

Sami's chin went up. The man knew how to raise nerves. Light years ago, a hungry thirteen-year-old runaway had promised herself that she would never be scared again. Sami had kept that promise. She might not like the man, but she certainly wasn't frightened of him.

She closed the door, locked it, and leaned against it, then laced her fingers behind her hips. "You are not going anywhere, Mr. Woden."

Over the breadth of a leather-covered shoulder, he drew his brows together as he turned fully toward her. His deep-set lids opened . . . fractionally. He peered at her.

"I'm not?" His deep drawl mocked her.

"No. Not yet, anyway." Sami knotted the belt tighter about her small waist. "I'll make coffee; then we'll talk this thing over like two civilized adults."

His slate-colored eyes slid over the red plaid robe as she walked past him to the kitchen. He straightened to his full height and snaked out a hand. It looped about

Sami's upper arm and drew her back to stand before him.

"No prim little snip of a schoolteacher orders me around, Miss Sass. Even one with eyes as big and brown as yours." The slash between his brows and the brackets about his firm mouth deepened as he glared down at her.

Sami slowly, firmly freed her arm from his grip. "I'm simply inviting you to share a cup of coffee, Mr. Woden," she said smoothly. "Shall I make it, or not?"

The rough-hewn rancher stared at her as if she were a timber rattler coiled for the strike. A long moment ticked by as his stare prowled her face, gauged the mettle beneath the brown velvet eyes. His eyes traced the upturned nose and the full curve of her mouth as though he were seeing her for the first time.

"Damn. You *do* starch your panties," he drawled, then gave a slow smile.

Sami's retort caught on her tongue as she spied the deep gash that crossed his left temple. It was fresh; there was dried blood around it. Without thinking, she raised a finger and traced the two-inch line on the weathered skin. "What happened to your head?"

Woden's rugged face dipped to just inches above hers. His hand wrapped about the slenderness of her wrist to hold it loosely. The rough pad of his thumb stroked the silken flesh covering the thin blue veins. Sami's flesh heated as the pendulum stroke quickened. Mesmerized, she could not move.

He smelled of bourbon and smoke and of musky after shave and the earthy scent of man.

He raised his other hand, paused in midair by her face, then let it slide into the thickness of her hair. His large thumb continued its slow stroke as he stared down at his fingers winnowing through the long strands.

"It's black as a crow's wing . . ." The husky depth of his voice raised the fine hairs at the back of her neck.

His tones seemed to weave a silken web about her, melding the soles of her bare feet to the cool linoleum.

An unfathomable expression crossed his face. "You're as pretty as a newborn calf, lady. How old are you?"

The raw sound of her own swallow brought Sami to reality. She slid from Woden's grasp, allowing a long swathe of hair to veil the flush warming her face. He had reached into her innermost core and tugged strings. She did not want those emotions uncovered, did not want the pain of loving again. Yet her body responded to the lean, masculine length of his; her breasts were sensitized beneath the T-shirt.

Sami tried to remember what the thread of the conversation had been before Ben had touched her. Methodically, she filled the aluminum coffee pot with water, measured in the grounds, and capped it. She turned on the burner, and flames leaped, sputtering as they touched the water droplets on the bottom of the pot.

Woden's boot heel tattooed the worn carpet in a steady beat as the silence grew. Finally, he cleared his throat. "Look, ma'am. I shouldn't have come here tonight. But Mike and me . . . well, we argued. Yelled at each other, I mean. He's just as ornery-tempered as his old man, I guess." He hesitated, and the boot heel's tempo increased. "Like I said when I came in, deal's off," he added roughly. "I'd better be on my way."

Sami's thoughts cleared suddenly. She wanted the job Woden had offered. She had to keep him here until she had firmly reinstated herself as his son's tutor.

She leaned a hip against the kitchen counter and crossed her arms over her chest. "Stay where you are, Mr. Woden. You woke me out of a perfectly good sleep, and I don't like being awakened by some pie-eyed cowboy without good cause."

Woden's brows lifted, surprise written across his dark expression.

"I've just started coffee, and it would be impolite of you to leave now." She glanced at his grim mouth, then checked the perking coffee. "My, that smells good. Sit on the couch, Mr. Woden, and I'll serve."

It began low, like a mountain cat's purr, then erupted into an emphatic curse. "I'm not in the mood for coffee, lady."

Sami's eyes widened. She fluttered her lashes. "Really? Well, *I* wasn't in the mood to wake up so early. But here we are, aren't we? Cream? Sugar?"

"Black," he growled.

"You might as well take off your hat and sit down, Mr. Woden. You look uncomfortable." Actually, he looked like a Brahma bull ready to come out of the rodeo chute.

The couch creaked, and Sami glanced into the living room. Woden's weight made the battered cushion sag. His hat lay on the seat beside him, and his long legs were stretched out before him, his forearms resting on his thighs. His dark head was bowed as if he were studying his hands.

She walked toward him carrying two mugs. When he looked up, she saw the deep lines of fatigue about his eyes and the dark circles beneath him. He took a mug and balanced it on his knee. "Thanks."

She settled into the semicircle of a chair and drew her legs beneath her, then tucked the robe about her feet and cupped her mug with both hands. After he took his first sip, she asked quietly, "How did you get the cut on your temple, Mr. Woden?"

"'Mr. Woden,'" he mumbled. "Sounds like my father, not me."

He sprawled against the couch back, rested his head on it. "When Mike threw the book, I didn't duck fast enough." His eyelids closed, and he breathed deeply.

"You said he didn't like the idea of me tutoring him this summer. Is that right?" Sami ventured.

"At this point, Mike doesn't like anyone or anything.

It was a stupid idea, I guess. Hell, I thought some good might come of it."

Sami blew the steam from her coffee and took a small sip. "Drink your coffee, Mr. Woden. Please," she urged softly.

"Yeah. Then I'll be on my way." He half rose, sipped the brew, then lowered his head against the couch. "Damn, I'm tired. I don't know which one pitched the biggest fit today, the Baron or Mike."

He leaned forward, his hands cupping the mug between the spread of his thighs. "Look, I'm sorry I woke you up. I'd had a few drinks, and it was a long day, okay?" The apology slid through his lips reluctantly.

Sami met his stare. "No, it's not okay. I'm holding you to your deal. We shook on it. Remember?"

He shook his craggy head from side to side as though erasing her words. "What did you say?"

"I said I'm holding you to your deal. My nieces are excited about going to the ranch, and we're all packed. I've already spent a lot of your money, Mr. Woden. I intend to earn it."

"I thought that was what you said," he said slowly. "What are you . . . just past five foot? A hundred, hundred-ten pounds dripping wet? And what . . . twenty-four, twenty-five at the most?" He sat the mug on the end table, and his raw-boned wrists rested on his knees, hands loose.

"I've dealt with problem teenagers before, and I have references if you require them. And I'm thirty-two."

"Mike's almost a man. That book would have knocked you silly, half-pint. And I'd have been responsible."

Sami aimed and took her best shot. "Are you a quitter, Mr. Woden?"

Bull's-eye!

The small room seemed to tilt at a forty-five-degree angle. A muscle jerked in his cheek, and a throbbing cord ran from beneath his ear to the gray and black hair nestled in the opening of his collar. The only sound in the room was that of his slow, heavy breathing as he stared at her.

"Not that I remember, little bit," he drawled. "I have a few belts down me, and I may be sleeping on my feet. But if I were you . . ." The gray eyes scalded her. "Just don't push me."

Mary Jane's frightened call penetrated the charged silence. "Aunt Sami! Where are you?"

Sami set her mug next to Woden's and uncurled her legs to stand. Woden's thunderous expression didn't change as he watched her.

"I have to assure my nieces that everything is all right, Mr. Woden. They frighten easily, and it may take a little time to put them back to sleep. Are you going to run away?"

The set of his jaw shifted as he mumbled a curse. "Damn, you've got nerve."

"I'll be back as soon as I can," Sami promised. "Make yourself comfortable."

Sami disengaged herself a second time from the tangle of young limbs. She crawled over Mary Jane's body and stood beside the bed. Rays of dawn came through the window and touched the two dark heads, making the black curls shine.

"Everything is going to be just fine, babies." She tugged the quilt higher about them, patted each child as she snuggled down in the bed. "Go to sleep now."

When she returned to the living room, the rancher was asleep. His tall body was stretched out on the couch, head resting on one upholstered arm, sock-covered feet stretched past the other. He had draped the leather jacket over the discarded boots.

Sami clicked off the lamp and stood beside him. Sleep had eased the hardness from his expression, the fringe of his lashes creating spiked shadows over the stubble-covered cheeks. Slightly parted, his lips were fuller. The top one was no more than a length of curved line, but the lower one . . .

She leaned closer, watching the easy flow of his breath lift and lower his chest. The pearl snaps of his shirt were opened to his waist now. The hair covering his chest was more black and less gray as it tapered to his belt buckle. He shifted, the couch creaked, and the shirt fell away from one side of his chest. Sami studied the dark nipple, unable to look away.

"Come here, little bit." Two arms wrapped about her, hauling her down beside him. A heavy thigh clamped over her legs, locking them immobile.

Shackled by the strength of his body, her head tucked beneath his chin, Sami squirmed but could not dislodge his hold. "Mr. Woden!"

"I've watched that pretty little mouth talk and wondered how your lips would taste, half-pint," he murmured. "I bet they're as sweet as the high-meadow flowers."

"Mr. Woden!" Sami's arms were pinned to her sides, her nose tucked into the hollow at the base of his neck. The strong thighs stopped her legs before they could escape. A callused hand cupped her jaw, tilting her face toward his lips.

"Mmmm." Sami's protest slid back into her throat, muffled by the urgent pressure of his lips.

A heartbeat later, he murmured against her mouth, "Easy now, little bit. Easy. I won't hurt you."

His mouth teased hers. Tantalizing kisses prowled the soft contours of her lips. For a moment, Sami watched the closed lids so near her face. As his mouth played tenderly on hers, Sami felt her taut body yield to the mellow warmth, easing her curves to fit the hard lines of his body.

Her eyes closed as one large hand followed the length of her spine slowly. Down . . . up. Each descent took his palm lower on the gentle rise of her bottom.

His other hand filtered the long strands tangling around her neck, then lifted them behind her. Warm and rough and exciting, his thumb stroked the hollow at the base of her throat.

His lips teased and parted hers, then tugged at her lower lip, sucking it gently into his mouth. Eventually, he freed and kissed it.

Sami fell, soared, floated with his caresses. Absorbed by the tenderness of his touch, the slight trembling of his body became her own. One thought entered her dream—she felt warm and lovely, as though he were wooing her. Her fingers found his belt and clung to it as he shifted her more comfortably against him.

She lifted her lips to the ones plaguing hers, hungry now for each light caress. The hand on her back cradled the fullness of one hip, turned her against his hard body.

Sami's sigh raised her breasts against the width of his chest, and they ached, sensitized and full.

Against her mouth, he murmured, "I feel it, too, sweetheart."

His fingers eased aside the flannel lapel of her robe, then slid lower to cup the weight of one breast. Through the cotton T-shirt, his thumb teased her nipple gently, then slipped to the other one and shaped it with his palm.

No longer floating, Sami yielded to her desire. It had been so long since she had touched a man . . . Her hands slipped beneath his shirt, stole quickly through the thick mat on his chest to find one dark nub. She explored it timidly as the large hand cupping her breast tightened and caressed the tender softness.

"So perfect. So small and complete. And sweet . . ." He groaned as he slid beneath her, lifting her on top of him. "So warm, honey . . ."

Cradled between his thighs, Sami pressed against him. Her hair draped about his head, tangling with the dark, crisp waves framing his face.

Through the window, the gray dawn touched the

angles of his face. She cupped the hard jaw with her palms, fingers splayed into the coarse texture of the waves by his temple. Her index finger ran lightly down the center of his face, tracing the heavy brow, the broken line of his nose, the indentation above his mouth, then the mouth itself.

Drawn by his parted lips, Sami inched her body higher on his. Her breasts flattened against him as she slid upward on the steel-hard chest. His hands lightly cupped her bottom as she placed her mouth on his. She tasted the bourbon, the smoke. And tasted the man.

She had to get closer. Locking her arms about his neck, she kissed him deeply, drugged by the feel of him beneath her.

Then Sami was suddenly aware of the firm hands at her waist. Slowly, gently, Woden eased her body from his own.

She lifted her head and questioned him silently with her eyes.

His left hand lifted the canopy of her hair, gathering it into a loose ponytail. "Whoa, little bit," he whispered, and tugged gently.

Dazed, wrapped in her own needs, she stared down at him.

"Slow down, honey," he urged, his right hand rubbing the small of her back. "Easy."

Cradled by his Levi-covered thighs, her own legs began to quiver. Her stomach knotted, reacting to her shaken emotions. Her breasts ached, and her fingertips trembled against his jaw.

His breath brushed her cheeks. "It's okay, sweetheart. I feel it, too. Hurt with it."

Sami barely heard the raw baritone as his breath swept over her face. "Don't look so shocked, honey. Come here . . ." He eased her shaking body downward, his hand resting on her hip. The other hand stroked her hair slowly, eased her head beneath his chin.

"You're an explosive little package," he rasped over her head.

Sami snuggled to the breadth of his chest, her fingers walking through the coarseness there. He captured her hand and held it within his. "Don't."

Beneath her cheek, his heart thumped heavily, its beat slowing. His arms tightened about her shaking body, held her easily. "You caught me by surprise, little bit." His voice was husky. "To sink into your soft little body would be the easiest thing in the world. Right now, I feel as though I've been stomped, but good."

The night air chilled her flesh, but Sami's face was hot with shame. She had all but ravished the man!

"I'm . . . I'm sorry," she croaked. "Of course this mustn't happen."

His chuckle feathered the tendrils framing her face. "I'm not sorry. No man in his right mind would be." He continued to rub her back. "Damn. I'm too old for rolling two to a couch. And too big." His tone sounded lazy and pleased.

Sami had to get away from him. Ben was not a safe person where her emotions were concerned. But as she tried to escape, his arms tightened. "Uh-uh," he said. "You're staying right here tonight. I may not know anything else now, but I know I need you next to me."

She cleared her throat, trying to find the words. "Mr. Woden, please let me go."

He gave a long, low chuckle.

"Shoot, ma'am. Call me Ben."

- 3 -

BEN CAME SLOWLY awake at the sound of a woman's soft voice.

"Girls, Mr. Woden won't feel well when he wakes up. It's best to let him sleep for a while." He heard the distant rattle of dishes over the sound of his own blood pounding against his skull. He shifted the length of his body and found that the lumps beneath him were no more accommodating than the rocks of a rodeo arena. A lightweight blanket covered him.

He recognized the woman's Arkansas accent. Sami. All prim and proper as a maiden schoolmarm, with enough backbone to match an army drill sergeant. He remembered the feel of her in his arms, and that his last coherent thought before drifting into sleep had been that she was one hell of a loving woman. A man should move heaven and earth to keep a woman like that beside him.

"Eat your oatmeal, Lori." Sami's voice floated over him like warm satin. He remembered the hungry strain of her body against him, the urgent hunger of her sweet lips.

"Yes, you can ride a horse, Mary Jane. Just you wait, baby. We're going to have fun. We'll play cowboys . . ." Ben half listened to her hushed singsong, thinking more clearly now about Sami Lassiter. Beneath her bluenose manners, she was dynamite. The top of her head barely reached his chest, but every satiny inch of her was all woman. Silky black hair, and skin as smooth as a baby's. Her soft breasts had filled his hands just right, and he still tasted the honeyed sweetness of her mouth as his tongue swept across his dry bottom lip.

"He's awake, Auntie. He's just playing 'possum," a child stated next to him. "How long before you get up, Mr. Woden?"

"I want to ride a horse, Mr. Woden," insisted a second child as Ben slowly forced open his lids. Sunlight seemed to blare into the room, hitting the back of his brain with all the impact of a sledgehammer.

"Mary Jane. Lori," Sami called softly from the kitchen. "You come away from there now. Mr. Woden will wake up soon enough."

"His eyes are open now, Auntie," one of the black-haired, brown-eyed little girls insisted. Ben closed his lids against the throb at the back of his head, then opened them slowly.

Dressed in a long-sleeved white sweater and navy slacks, Sami stood an arm's length away from him. Her hands rested on the little girls' shoulders. Her hair was tightly pinned on top of her head and secured by tortoiseshell combs.

Painfully, Ben eased himself up to a sitting position. When he chanced a glance at Sami's face, he found the censure he'd expected to see there. Behind her enormous glasses, the molten heat of her dark brown eyes flicked contemptuously over him. The haughty tilt of her upturned nose indicated that she found his presence less than desirable. The dimple in the center of her chin deepened as her incredibly soft lips pressed together.

He hadn't noticed before, but she wore no makeup. Her skin was as light and fresh-looking as cow's cream, her lips as velvety and dewy as rose petals. She was poised now and in charge of her emotions. But last night the composure had slipped to reveal volcanic passions. He felt an aching tension that began in the pit of his stomach and throbbed down his legs, reminding him of the intensity of his arousal a few hours ago. At the same time, his hangover thudded against his skull.

"The bathroom is down the hall. Everything you need is there," she said. The condemnation sharpening her soft voice snagged on his raw nerves. "Coffee will be ready when you're through. Come on, Mary Jane, Lori. Let Mr. Woden clean up. Come away now."

As she turned and urged the girls into the kitchen, Ben smelled her clean scent. It reminded him of the honeysuckle vines clinging to his front porch. He watched her hips sway gently within the fashionable slacks. For a small woman, she possessed long, shapely legs. His stomach wrenched as he remembered the press of them against his own. He swallowed. Damn.

Later, showered and feeling less ragged around the edges, Ben carefully placed his coffee mug on the kitchen table. Sami had caught him off stride last night, he decided. Her blazing sensuality had winded him for the moment.

He frowned so hard it hurt. He didn't like her high-handed attitude this morning. He liked a woman who knew the score and left well enough alone. And if he wanted loving for the night, he'd pick a female who was adult-sized.

He eyed the way her slender fingers curled around her cup, the precise manner in which she fitted the bottom of the cup into the saucer's identation. He liked his life the way it was now, on his terms. But Sami made him feel hot, sixteen, and tenderly possessive. His reaction to her sensuality was disconcerting for an experienced man of his age. He didn't want her around him. "You're not coming."

Across the table, Sami stared at him calmly. Her long lashes shadowed the coffee-colored depths of her eyes. The baby-soft ivory cheeks remained untinged by the flush he had somehow expected. Maybe she hadn't heard him. "You're not coming," he repeated.

"As I told you last night, Mr. Woden, I intend to make good my debt to you."

Her cool insistence irritated him. Ben narrowed his eyes, attempting to pierce the tinted lenses shielding her eyes. "Last night should have told you something, woman." Couldn't she see the danger of being near him? He still wasn't certain how he'd managed to rein the passion between them. "I've got my ways. I don't like changes. You wouldn't like it on the ranch."

"I am not going to debate the matter with you, Mr. Woden." He noted that her eyes were as soft as a fawn's.

"Ben," he insisted as he watched the tip of her tongue flick over her upper lip. Such an incredibly sensual mouth.

"When can we leave, Mr. Woden? Ben," she corrected.

He liked the slow, musical softness of her voice as she spoke his name. The sound of it settled over the dull throb in his head, and Ben forgot his objections. "As soon as I can pack the Bronco," he heard himself say.

"That's the highway to Togwotee Pass, Mary Jane. You follow it and you'll wind up at Yellowstone National Park watching Old Faithful erupt," Ben said over his shoulder to the excited girls. "Togwotee Pass was first an Indian trail, one of six that led to a trading hub, a city now called Jackson Hole. U.S. Highway two eighty-seven follows that old Indian trail."

Sami glanced at his rugged profile, mildly surprised

as he patiently answered the girls' excited questions. Pleasure rumbled through his deep voice as though he enjoyed sharing his wild mountain country with them.

"There's snow on the mountains, Mr. Woden. Could we go sledding up there?" asked Mary Jane.

His easy chuckle bounced against Sami's raw nerves. She had to admit that it cost her a measure of peace to hold her own with the abrupt rancher.

"That would be one heck of a sled ride," he said. "Togwotee Pass is almost ten thousand feet high and sometimes gets a hundred and twenty inches of compacted snow in the winter."

Lori flopped her doll across the broad width of his shoulder. She studied the mountains, holding the doll. Sami lifted it to her lap. "Don't distract Mr. Woden while he's driving, honey."

Across the distance of the seat, Ben glared at her, his eyebrows locked together. Ben Woden had a hangover and was as edgy as a grizzly, but he still managed to answer the girls' endless questions patiently. Yet for the past hour, each time *she* spoke, he'd glowered menacingly at her.

He obviously did not have the ability to communicate with her in a civilized manner. He was definitely too physical, exuding elemental maleness from every fiber of his tall, well-muscled body. She slanted a veiled glance down his Levi's and admitted to having felt a certain passing arousal last night. She was only a mortal woman, after all. And Ben did possess a certain . . . beefcake attraction. But his abrasive personality scuttled his appeal.

Her fingers searched for the security of her wedding ring. She had fallen into the habit of twisting it around her finger when she was under stress. But the ring was stored safely in the bank's security vault for the summer. Now she missed the reminder of the man she had loved.

Ben Woden was another matter. He practically

snarled at her. Whatever his problem was, she decided to let him simmer for the day. She asked lightly, "How did Wyoming get its name, Mr.—Ben?"

A muscle shifted in the rock-hard jaw; he seemed to chew her words thoroughly before spitting out the answer. "The name comes from a Delaware Indian word, Mechewe-ami-ing or M'cheuwomink. Means 'at the big plains,' or 'on the great plain.' "

"Will we see some Indians, Mr. Woden?" Mary Jane asked.

"Uh-huh. My son, Mike, is half Indian. His mother was from the Wind River Reservation." He glanced at Sami, and she felt something flicker over him. It was too quick to be named, yet too intense to dismiss. It jarred the smoothness she liked in her life.

"Gosh." Mary Jane's tone was wistful. "I wish I was an Indian."

"Hold on. This is where we leave the highway. It gets rough after this," Ben cautioned as he slowed and eased the Bronco through a small gulley. Concentrating on the ruts and the rocky road, he cursed beneath his breath.

His big hands tightened on the steering wheel, his knuckles whitening with tension. The front left tire sank into a deep rut, then lurched out of it. Sami was flung against the seat, her hands flailing to find security. Her right hand gripped an armrest, but the fingers of her left hand clamped over the muscles of Ben's hard thigh. He grunted and shot an impatient glance at her white face, then down at her hand gripping his upper thigh. The Bronco lurched to a stop in the middle of the evergreen-framed road.

Sami jerked her hand from his thigh and stiffly laced her cold fingers on her lap. She still felt the movement of Ben's well-developed leg muscles beneath her palm as he braked. She avoided the blaze of his eyes as she looked at Mary Jane and Lori. "Are you all right, girls?"

"Why are we stopping?" Lori asked fearfully.

Before Sami could ask the same question, Ben reached behind him to open a back door. "We're taking a break, girls. We've been driving for an hour, and it'll be another hour before we reach the ranch. Get out and play a little bit, but stay where we can see you."

As the children scampered from the confinement of the four-wheeler, Sami searched for her seat-belt latch. "Stay where you are, woman," Ben growled. His left hand gripped the steering wheel, but his right one held the belt crossing her chest.

The back of his hand brushed the skin at the base of her neck, and Sami instantly flattened herself against the seat behind her, her fingers locking about his to pry them free.

Ben's harsh face loomed over her, the lines deepening beside his mouth when Sami shivered.

"Well, I'll be." Ben heard his own amazed whisper as he realized Sami's reaction to his touch was one of fear. He'd seen it in the eyes of trapped animals. Stark naked fear. Because *he* had touched her!

He let go of the safety belt and saw a lessening of the wide-eyed panic behind the oversized glasses. He reached into the glove compartment for a pack of cigarettes left over from his smoking days. Lighting one, he watched Sami follow the movements of his hands.

He drew deeply on the cigarette, testing the tobacco before he blew smoke out the open window. The cigarette was stale, the package long forgotten in the Bronco. But Sami's reaction to his touch was enough to cause any man to break his vow to quit smoking. "I wouldn't hurt you, little bit. You look the way I felt one time when a Brahma bull the size of a house cornered me in a rodeo chute before the gate opened. Simmer down."

He relaxed into the seat, and through the windshield watched the children build a mound of pine cones. From the corner of his eye, he saw Sami's small hands grip each other; her tapered well-trimmed fingers twined restlessly. Such soft little hands. "Take a few deep breaths. It'll help."

After a moment of silence, he turned to her. Sami's eyes were closed, her head supported by the headrest behind her. She swallowed, and he thought how easily he could circle her neck with one hand. Color had eased back into her face and the creamy skin now bore a flush. He longed to loosen the tightly knotted mass of hair, run his fingers through the long, scented tresses as he kissed her fear away.

"I didn't imagine what happened last night, Sami," he said, speaking roughly to counter the path his thoughts wanted to take. "You let me touch you then, and more. Now you act as though I'd tried to hurt you. I can almost hear your heart pound."

Beneath the white sweater, her breasts rose and fell in a deep sigh. Her eyelids drifted open and haunted brown velvet eyes stared back at him. "You're absolutely right," she admitted tiredly. "I overreacted just now. I'm sorry."

Ben's heart thumped unevenly. *Why had she overreacted?* He caught Lori's happy wave and returned it automatically, his mind on the woman beside him. He wanted her reason. "Will you tell me why?"

Her voice, hesitant and hushed, swept over to him. "Maybe you *should* know, since we'll be in the same household. It would only be fair to tell you; it could happen again." She took a deep breath, staring dully at a cottontail rabbit zigzagging across the rutted road. Ben watched the rabbit disappear into a thick stand of lodgepole pine and sumac as he waited for her to speak.

"It happened a long time ago." She sighed, then continued, "A big man hurt me." She winced as she remembered her father's abuse, then shrugged. "It comes back sometimes. When I least expect it. That's all that happened just now."

Anger ran through Ben like wildfire. "I see," he said

slowly. "I'm big, and when I reach toward you, you . . ." He couldn't finish the rest of the sentence.

"Exactly. Don't worry, Ben." The soft lips attempted a smile that did not completely curve upward before it died. "It doesn't happen very often."

"We're in a hell of a fix," Ben stated bluntly. He wanted to hold her in his arms, to protect her, to make love to her until the fear was buried.

Sami smoothed a wispy tendril of hair behind her ear and patted it into place. Her chin rose higher as she straightened and said, "I don't see any problem."

"I do. Mike's temper matches mine."

"I can handle him. I'm qualified, Mr.—Ben."

"Qualified!" he snorted. "You're half the size of him."

Sami adjusted her glasses with the tip of her finger. "Size has nothing to do with it. Teaching skill does," she said firmly, quietly.

Ben looked at her steadily. Cool, in charge of her emotions, Sami unwaveringly met his gaze. "Shall we go?"

He raked his fingers through his hair. Sami Lassiter might be pocket-sized, but she had a will of concrete. "Dammit, you're not listening."

"I can take care of myself. And *you* are to stop cursing. I won't allow it around the children."

When Ben drove around the last bend in the road before his ranch, the girls spotted horses grazing on the rich plateau grass. "A horsey! We want to ride the horses!" they chorused from the back seat.

The Woden ranch house spread across a small clearing. Nestled in the pine forest, the two-story log and shingle structure looked as though it belonged to the previous century. It seemed as though any moment a fur-capped and leather-swathed trapper might wander out to the wide porch.

Ben parked the Bronco near the foot of the wooden

steps. "It's not as primitive as it looks. But we've only got one bathroom—haven't needed another one," he said gruffly. He slid from the seat, crossed in front of the vehicle, and opened the door for the children. He lifted them down, then opened Sami's door. "Come on. Get out."

He stretched out a hand to help her to the ground. Then, as if remembering her reaction to his touch, he withdrew his hand. His tall body tensed, the line of his jaw hardening.

Sami would not allow this cowboy to intimidate her, nor would she give in to her fears. Deliberately, she extended her hand and waited for him to take it.

Ben stared at her hand for a long moment, then slowly placed his rough one beneath it, palm upward. His fingers trembled as they wrapped about hers, and his massive shoulders tensed beneath the leather jacket, yet his grip was light. Stiffly, he waited until she slipped to the ground, then jerked his hand free. Sami felt a smile tug on her lips. Somewhere inside cowboy Ben Woden there lurked a minimal knowledge of how to treat a lady. He regarded her warily.

"The house is so big, Aunt Sami," Lori breathed beside her, and she took the girl's hands in hers.

Ben cleared his throat. "The place is cool in the summer, and we've got modern conveniences. If you need something else, I'll get it for you," he said defensively.

Sami looked straight up into his steel-gray eyes. "Everything will be just fine, Ben."

"Damn, I hope you're right, Sami." The lines deepened about his eyes as he peered down at her. "You've bitten off quite a hunk."

A huge Saint Bernard rounded the corner of the house at a lope. His huge paws hit Ben's back, and the rancher chuckled as he turned to scratch the enormous dog's ears. "I'm glad to see you, too, Chug. Ladies, this is Chugalug. He likes beer."

"Emma," he called before opening the back panel of the Bronco and lifting out several cardboard boxes.

"Don't yell, Ben. I'm right here." A rotund gray-haired woman with an enormous apron covering her floral-print dress stepped onto the wooden porch. The screen door behind her almost closed on a thin, stooped man whose face bore as many lines as a Wyoming road map.

"I'm Emma, the housekeeper," the woman stated as she bounced down the steps, her husband following in her wake. "And this here's my husband, Dan. We live in the cabin out back. You must be the schoolteacher for Mike. Well, you got your job cut out for you. Are these your young 'uns? Hurry up, Ben. Stop lollygagging around and get those boxes up to the young 'uns' room. Chug, don't you jump on the poor babies, now. Oh, they're such skinny little things. I got a big pot of chicken and noodles for lunch, and then I imagine the missy will want to put the children down for naps. Come on, now, get moving. Dan, you help him."

The older man stood next to his wife and studied Sami. The wrinkles in his brow deepened. "Ain't much to her, Ben," he stated as he stopped to lift a box from the vehicle before disappearing into the house.

"Shush, now, Dan," ordered his wife as she met Lori's and Mary Jane's timid smiles. "Come on, girls. I baked a chocolate cake especially for you." She took the girls' hands and led them up the stairs to the front door, chattering as they entered the house.

"Emma talks a lot. Too much," Ben grumbled as he hefted a large box under each arm.

"I think I like her," Sami said as she reached inside the tailgate to pick up a box.

"Leave it, woman. It's bigger than you are," Ben ordered brusquely. The tone of his voice raised Sami's hackles, and she turned to glare at him. His black brows met savagely over smoldering gray eyes. "Come on. Emma doesn't like to keep meals waiting."

She didn't like his commanding tone, but Sami decided to ignore it . . . this first day anyway. Ben Woden needed to improve his bunkhouse manners, she decided as she followed his broad shoulders, lean hips, and long legs up the steps. She sidestepped Chug's huge paws as the dog frolicked like a puppy about his owner's legs.

Ben shouldered open the plank door and allowed Sami to enter the huge room in front of him. Multicolored rugs covered the wooden floor; a bearskin lay before a massive rock fireplace. The room was starkly masculine from the well-stocked gun case to the huge leather couch and matching chairs.

Chug ran past them, skidded on a braided rug, and bumped into a wall. Panting, his tongue hanging out, he stared at them solemnly from beneath the layers of wrinkles on his brow.

"Just follow the chattering and you'll find the kitchen," Ben said near her. "Dan and I will take your things upstairs."

"When will I meet Mike?" Sami asked as he started toward the stairway.

"I'm here, teach." From the depths of the couch rose a young man as tall as his father, yet lacking Ben's muscled breadth. His complexion was darker, his long black hair bound at the base of his neck by a leather string. He sauntered around the couch to Sami, his thumbs hooked the pockets of his jeans as his jet-black eyes appraised her.

"I'm glad to meet you, Mike." Sami extended her hand, but the young man just looked at it, his mouth curling into a sneer. Over her head Ben growled, "Shake Ms. Lassiter's hand, Mike."

Mike flashed an insincere grin at his father. "Sure, Dad. She's a little different from your usual, isn't she?"

Ben's features hardened. "Don't get cute."

"I don't need a teacher, Dad. Much less one half the size of Chug. I'm too old for this junk, and all my friends think it's—"

"Don't say it, Mike," Sami interrupted softly, and both men looked down at her as though she'd just arrived on earth from another galaxy. She smiled at the younger man. "You're not afraid of me, are you?"

Mike's raven eyebrows shot up almost to his hairline. "Me? Afraid?"

She shrugged. "I hope not. Still, if you're not willing to try. . ." Sami watched the boy's expression settle into mulish lines before she prompted, "*Are* you willing to try, Mike?"

The boy looked at his father, then down at her. "I'm not afraid of anything, Ms. Lassiter." He drew a deep breath and exhaled sharply. "I'll give it a shot. But for how long?"

Sami extended her hand again. "Day by day. We start in the morning, nine o'clock sharp. Shake?"

Mike shook her hand, grumbling, "Okay. But I'm not afraid."

"The girls' bedroom is just next door. Mike's is across the hallway. My room is downstairs, and so is my study." Over the width of his shoulder, Ben stared down at Sami; his brows became a single black line. "Don't mess around in my study. I run my businesses from it. It's off limits."

He set the two boxes on top of a quilt-covered brass bed, then turned to Sami. "If you think Mike's decided to get his GED, after all, you're mistaken. He's hardheaded." He paused, then continued, "I work this ranch with Mike and Dan, more for pleasure than money; I run and breed a few cows while my broker and business manager tangle with investments. Mike has the choice of working with you or being shipped off to a private boys' school. For the moment, he's chosen you. But I won't stay in the house baby-sitting all day. You'll have to see that he studies."

"No one's asking you to baby-sit—Mr. Woden," Sami stated quietly, using the formal address for effect.

"In fact, I intend to have regular study hours and prefer that you not interrupt them. Unless, of course, you want to study for your general equivalency diploma, too. I could easily teach *two* older students."

"Hell! I'll be damned if I'll go back to school at my age," Ben exploded. "Listen, half-pint, you'd better walk lightly around me after last night."

At the open window, the cool mountain air fluttered the cotton curtains, but an equatorial storm brewed inside Sami. She dug her nails into the heels of her hands as she met his heated stare. How could one man raise her temperature just by uttering a few words? "I prefer to forget whatever you think may have happened last night, Mr. Woden. You were drunk. And I've asked you before to watch your language."

The black and gray tuft of hair escaping his collar rose as Ben inhaled sharply. "This is my house," he stated. "I talk how I want to. When you decide to take me on, come ahead, half-pint." His large hand reached out to snag her wrist; firm fingers encircled it and drew her to him, just as his other arm closed about her.

"And last night *did* happen, little bit," he murmured before his mouth descended on hers. Sami's surprised gasp was smothered by his lips.

His firm mouth touched, lifted, then trailed across her bottom lip. She felt the roughness of his indrawn breath as it pressed his chest to her breasts. One hand freed her wrist and slid up to the back of her head as the other splayed across her lower back and drew her body to his. As his hard mouth slanted more fully on the softness of hers, Sami could not protest, could not force inches between his body and hers.

"Come here, woman," he breathed against the smoothness of her cheek. "Hell, I need this. I didn't dream last night; I wasn't that drunk. I know I held you and I know you moved against me with all the heat of a pine-forest fire."

Taken unaware, Sami floated as one large hand

stroked her spine, settled above the curve of her buttocks, then edged lower to cup her fullness. The warmth of his other hand matched the first as he eased her up into the hard cradle of his hips. Sami's toes left the floor as Ben's strong arms once more slid around her. Braced against the lean strength of his body, she somehow did not care. She wanted to feel Ben's heart racing against her own, wanted the solid male thrust imprinted against the restlessness of her hips. She pressed her palms against the steely heat of his chest, smoothing the fabric before sliding her hands to lock her fingers behind his neck.

Her softness flattened against the rigid planes of his chest as she hungrily sought his lips with her own. His upper arms pressed against the outer perimeter of her soft breasts as Ben's large hands curved over her hips. His breath swept her cheek, hot and urgent, as his head lowered.

For a millisecond, eyes the color of smoke stared into hers. Then his eyelids slowly closed and his mouth captured her waiting lips. The rough growl caught low in his throat, vibrating against her softness before he ordered, "Open them, little bit. Let me in."

When Sami's lips parted, his tongue slid into the moist warmth, searching the sweetness until her tongue timidly returned the love play. Pressed against the urgent male outline of Ben's hips, Sami felt a hunger grow low in her abdomen. She wanted—needed—to make love, to be fully a woman once more.

Ben growled once more, sweeping his right arm beneath her knees to lift her against his chest. With Sami in his arms, he sat on the bed, cradling her on his lap. His left arm braced her back, the fingers of his right hand tugged at the sweater until it came free of her slacks. "Just keep holding me, little bit. Just keep holding me . . ." he murmured as wildfire spread through Sami.

"Easy, honey." The roughened hand swept downward. Gently, the heel of his palm rested on one hip-bone. The tips of his long fingers slowly traced the jut of the other bone. "You're shaking. Easy," he whispered raggedly against her temple as the palm of his hand trailed down one slender thigh, then the other.

Unable to wait for his kiss, Sami turned toward him. Her hands clasped the rugged contours of his jaw to urge the return of his mouth. Gently, his tongue traced the fullness of her lips, flicked the sensitive corners before playing with the other side of her mouth. His hand, rough and hard, slipped beneath her sweater and caressed its way upward to release the front hook of her bra. His trembling fingertips rested in the valley between her breasts, pressed on either side by the sensitive, aching weight.

His body shook, and within the circle of her arms, his brawny shoulders tensed. He nuzzled the tender skin beneath her ear, his ragged breath sweeping down the length of her neck as his coarse fingertips prowled the satin-smooth texture of her aching breasts. "Little bit, little bit . . ." he groaned as another tremor racked his hardened body.

"Ben . . ." She wanted that large hand over her breasts, needed it.

"Honey, you're one hell of a firecracker," he breathed huskily into the coils of her ear. His hand slipped downward, then withdrew from her sweater. He adjusted the knit fabric gently about her waistline. "I'll bet you didn't take your husband's temper lying down."

Her husband's temper? Des had been a gentle man, a friend. What was Ben referring to? When Sami silently questioned him with her eyes, Ben took her left hand in his. He rested their joined hands on her lap as his right hand pressed her head to the hard pad of his shoulder. He rocked her gently. "I need to know about him, honey.

"You jumped like you'd been bitten by a snake when I touched you during the trip home. He was the big man who hurt you, wasn't he?" He rolled her ring finger gently between his thumb and index finger. "There's an untanned line around your finger as though you've just removed a wedding band." His voice contained an accusation; Ben didn't like the pale mark on her flesh.

Sami's aching body floated back into reality, the sensual mists lifting. Held like a child on the rough-hewn rancher's lap, she felt the heat of embarrassment replace the flush of desire. Ben had the physical ability to make her want him, but he also possessed the means to cool her rising desire. *What was she doing?*

Ben lifted her glasses from her nose and carefully placed them on the hand-sewn quilt. With the tip of one finger, he tilted up her face for his perusal. The rough pad of his thumb prowled over the dimple in the center of her chin as he asked, "Are you still married?"

Sami closed her eyes, unable to face the silent inquisition in Ben's face. Her love for Des had been deeply fulfilling, their marriage was a very private memory. Ben probed too hard, too deep, into emotional territory that she did not want to reveal. He thought her husband had hurt her—but Des had been appalled by stories of her father's brutality. She would not explain the intricacies of her past life. "To satisfy your curiosity, I *was* married, but my husband never hurt me. Now, let me go."

"No." The sharpness of his tone and the strength of the hand gently shackling her wrists as she began to struggle infuriated Sami. "I was married twice, little bit. Once, as a boy, to Mike's mother—but she died when he was two. The next marriage seemed like a good idea at the time: We were good friends, and Mike needed a mother, I thought. Then someone else came along, and she found the love I couldn't seem to give her. We were still friends when I stepped aside. Now"—he drew a deep breath—"I want to know about the man who put his brand on you."

Once more Ben pried into her innermost emotions.

He had to have sensed that she did not want to discuss her marriage with him. He had no right to bore into her grief, disregarding her wishes.

Sami's anger vibrated through her bones, heated the blood rushing beneath her skin. Her frown tugged at the tight skin at her temples. Ben was the size of a mountain, and he stomped through her tattered emotions with all the sensitivity of his bull, the Baron. Des occupied a very special place in her heart; he had been a gentle man who didn't ask the wrong questions. He had listened, and he had understood.

Sami met Ben's eyes with her own. "You're my employer, Mr. Woden, but that doesn't give you the right to ask personal questions."

The thumb that warmed the dimple in her chin stopped, then lifted to trail across the softness of her bottom lip. Ben's sparkling gray eyes and deepening facial lines blended into a slow, white-toothed grin. "Shoot. I thought we *were* getting personal a minute ago, little bit."

His easy tone stoked Sami's temper, and she sought to control its eruption. "Emma is probably waiting for us."

"Yep. She gets mad as a banty hen when I'm late for a meal." He tapped the tip of her nose gently, then eased her off his lap and stood up. "But don't think the subject's forgotten. I mean to know everything about you, Samantha Lassiter. I already know that beneath those please-and-thank-you manners you're a bullheaded spitfire and a whole lot of woman," he said as he lifted her to her feet. "You also appear to be the kind of woman who likes things changed around to suit her. But if you have any ideas in that direction, forget them. I like my house the way it is: The furniture stays put, and Emma cooks food the way I like it. Mike may see things your way, and he might get his diploma; in fact, I pray he does. Other than that, things stay just the way they are."

"Fine." Sami didn't like the arrogant stance of his

well-developed legs or the confident tilt of the sable-haired head. Ben didn't spare any time for pleasantries, so why should she? "Mike will get his diploma, Mr. Woden. But in the meantime, the children and I will be living here, isn't that right?"

When he nodded slowly, she continued, "Then you must see that some changes will *have* to be made in your household."

"Such as?" he drawled warily.

"Well, where shall I teach? I'll need a room especially for that purpose, one without any distractions."

His eyebrows knit together, the deep-set eyes darkening stormily. His fingers scratched the mat at the base of his strong tanned neck as he thought. "This is no mansion. There's only one room private enough: my study."

"Can we use it?" Sami pressed. She felt a measure of satisfaction as the muscles bunched in his jaw and neck, as if he had to swallow something he didn't like.

He nodded reluctantly. "I do my business early in the morning and late at night. Use the room between those times. And take a message if my business manager calls," he ordered. "Try not to scare Banjo off. He's an ex–rodeo clown with a lot of business savvy." His gaze strolled lazily downward over her white sweater and navy slacks, then darkly pinned hers. "Banjo McGee's a pushover for kids and sweet little things like you. He turns into a two-hundred-fifty-pound marshmallow."

No danger of Ben Woden turning into a marshmallow, Sami thought ruefully as they went silently down to lunch.

- 4 -

EARLY THE NEXT morning, while the girls were snuggled in their new beds upstairs, Sami luxuriated in the privacy of the only bathroom in the Woden ranch house. She lifted her freshly washed hair with her fingers and aimed the blow-dryer with her other hand.

She sighed nostalgically as she remembered the beautiful bathroom Des had built for her with the payment for his first important art commission. The sunken tub, lush carpeting, and enormous vanity and mirrors contrasted to the sterility of this small, functional room with its medicine-cabinet mirror. Des had been soothing, sensitive to all her needs, while Ben's arrogance grated against every civilized fiber within her.

When her hip-length hair was dry, she tightened the loose flannel robe about her waist, unplugged the dryer, and took her bath powder and moisturizer from the small shelf below the mirror. Early-morning birdsong trilled outside the quietness of the rambling house as she opened the door.

Ben Woden, clad only in jeans, blocked her path. The hair-roughened breadth of his chest lifted and fell unevenly in front of her face. When she followed the darkly tanned column of his neck upward, she saw that the gray eyes were stormy and the sable waves were rumpled, touched by silver beneath the hallway light. Covered with blue-black stubble, his jaw jutted forward, resembling one of the carvings on Mount Rushmore. His teeth seemed to grind rhythmically to the tap of one large bare foot.

He scanned the clutter in her hands, regarding the dryer, powder, and toiletries with a deepening scowl. If his expression was any gauge, he might have been waiting in the hallway for hours.

In her present mood, Ben was as welcome as a carton of cracked eggs. "Good morning, Ben," she greeted him lightly, and moved to step by him. Leaning one tanned, brawny shoulder against the door frame, he crossed his arms over the width of his chest.

Blocking her passage, he stared down at her steadily, exuding a primitive heat that tingled down the length of Sami's freshly bathed body.

"Is something wrong, Mr. Woden?" she asked pleasantly. Did he have to begin the day with the aura of a wounded grizzly?

"You sing when you shower," he told her accusingly. "The blasted noise rips right through the walls into my room next door. It's a wonder everyone else is still asleep."

Sami stared at him. Ben could be held up as an object lesson in bluntness, but his barbs were not going to hook her into an unpleasant exchange. "I'll try to be quiet after this, Mr. Woden. Excuse me," she said as she made another attempt to pass him.

Ben did not shift his two-hundred-pounds-plus frame. The smile growing on his unshaven face was not cordial.

"Excuse me, please," Sami repeated more firmly.

She really did not want the anger beginning to simmer within her to come to a boil.

"There'd better not be any female paraphernalia cluttering up the place." He nodded toward the bathroom. "I don't plan to battle my way through a jungle of lace long johns every morning."

Sami could feel her temperature climbing to match the steamy heat of the room behind her. The tall rancher was deliberately picking a fight, and she was equally determined not to accommodate him. She did not like the strong emotions he could raise within her. "I have a busy day ahead, Mr. Woden. Will you please move aside?"

He reached out to trail a forefinger over a long lock of hair lying on her shoulder. "Maybe. You look about twelve now. Fuzzy and warm," he offered conversationally. "You smell good, too."

Sami felt the wooden planks slant beneath the soles of her bare feet. Ben could be as irritating as a willful child, but the sexy rumble of his voice and the glittering excitement beneath his lashes could be packaged and sold under the name Devastating Male.

He wound the strand of hair around his tanned finger, testing its texture with the pad of his thumb. The movement of his palm beside her cheek sent chills rippling through Sami. Instinctively, her head jerked away from the touch, and she thrust out the palm of her hand.

The blow caught Ben in his lean stomach. He reeled backward a step as Sami brushed by him. "Hey!" he yelled. "Pick on someone your own size!"

Later, in the book-lined study, Mike muttered, "This stuff is stupid."

Mentally, Sami compared the younger Woden's behavior to his father's. Abrasive, blunt, they both lacked the ability to sustain a polite conversation. The summer stretched out before her with all the enticement of a social desert. Inwardly, she sighed, remembering the pleasant times she had spent with Des, the quiet enjoyment as they discussed Van Gogh's techniques over shrimp-stuffed mushrooms. But aloud she said quietly, "I need to find out what you already know, Mike. We can do that easily enough this afternoon; then we can proceed from there. Also, we'll need to purchase the necessary books."

Lanky, dressed in a worn chambray shirt and dirty jeans, Mike glared at her. "What would it take for you to pass the exam for me?"

Sami sat back in Ben's huge desk chair and adjusted the cotton skirt about her legs, allowing her toes to dangle above the floor as she faced him. "Even if that were possible, you wouldn't want it, Mike."

The boy's high cheekbones and strong jaw promised to one day match the arrogance of his father's as he asked, "Hell, why not? Once the guys find out my old man hired me a nanny, I'll be the laughingstock of the country. None of the gang graduated, either." He shrugged. "Hey, look. I've got some money in my savings account. I'll give it to you if you'll just take your kids and get out. It's probably more money than Dad is paying you to stay."

She studied the sleek black hair, the rebellious expression for a moment. As yet, Mike had not displayed the violence toward her that Ben had feared. And after talking with the young man, she felt he deserved more credit than his father gave him. From his arguments, she sensed intelligence and a reasoning power uncommon in his age group. She also knew she was determined to earn the salary his father was paying her. "He's gone to a lot of trouble for you, Mike. You don't want to let him down, do you?" she asked.

"Let him down?" Mike sat up straight in the old wingback chair. "We fight all the time. We always have. I don't see where I owe him anything." The black brows became a single line across his brow, reminding Sami of his father. "This is a nowhere deal. Whoever heard of a guy my age having a private teacher, anyway? If Dad pulls any more of this stuff, I'll ship out."

Sami quietly closed the textbook on the desk. Mike was spoiling for a fight, and she felt up to giving him one this morning. She slipped off the chair, apparently sized to Ben's tall stature, and stood.

As she walked toward him, Mike's wary eyes traveled over her clothing. The high-buttoned, primose-colored blouse and trim navy skirt matched the sedateness of her practical, laced shoes. "Jeez, you even look like a teach," he grumbled as he glanced with distaste at her tightly knotted mass of black hair. "It must be a law or something that all of you teachers have buns on top of your heads and specs on your noses."

She allowed the smile within her to form on her lips. "Very colorful language, Mike. You should do well in English composition. If you're not too afraid to try," she added as she leaned back against the desk.

Mike shifted restlessly in his chair. "I'm not afraid. School's boring. That's why I quit. That's why the other guys quit. We like to hang out, we don't need school. We can make good money guiding deer and elk hunters in the fall. If Dad pushes me, I'll ship out and make it on my own."

He frowned at her. "This idea of Dad's is a real bummer. I don't know where he got it from, anyway. *He* didn't graduate, and he's got all sorts of business deals all over Wyoming. He's got shares in uranium and coal. Owns some condominiums in Casper. That red phone on the desk is a hot line to his broker."

"I'd like to make you a wager, Mike. Are you a gambler?"

He regarded her warily, yet Sami noticed a flickering of interest. "I've shot craps once or twice. What's the deal?"

"I'll bet that if you give me a chance, I can interest you in learning. In passing your GED."

"I don't know . . . I've offered to top the salary Dad's paying you to clear out. Why would you want to teach me, anyway? Not that I need it," he added.

Sami placed her glasses on the desk and rubbed the bridge of her nose. Mike had shown superior intelligence on the preliminary tests; he was too quick to fall for anything but the truth. "I know how hard it is to 'ship out,' as you said, Mike," she began.

"Yeah, sure. Tell me how it is," he jibed, yet the black eyes watched her.

"I *did* run away, Mike. It was a tough road, one I wouldn't want you to travel—"

"Is this the part where you tell me how good I've got it? How hard Dad's worked to make enough money to send me to college?" Mike interrupted scornfully.

Sami took a deep breath and played her trump card. "No. This is the part where we wager." Mike's betting chips were already on the table; she read it in the brightness of his eyes. "I'm wagering you'll pass the test for your GED. The question is, what do you want from me if I lose?"

Mike's brown finger tapped his forehead. "I'd better think about it for a while. Offhand, I think I'd like to see you play cowboy for a day. Get all sweaty and dirty. You look too cool, as though nothing ever burned your . . ." His grin was rueful as he added, "The back of a horse is a lot harder than a teacher's chair." As he stretched out his hand for hers, his half-smile held all the makings of the Woden male charm. "Bet?"

Sami's laughter erupted as she shook his hand. "You drive a hard bargain, partner."

The study door crashed open as Ben strode into the room. He glanced at their joined hands, then scowled at Sami. "I want a word with you, ma'am."

Mike squeezed her hand before his fingers slipped free. His raised eyebrows telegraphed "watch out" before he left the room. Ben closed the door behind his son, then stalked toward Sami. He snatched the battered hat from his head and slapped his thigh with it. A cloud of dust rose from his faded jeans; the upward sweep of the hat sent the cloud flying toward Sami.

He jammed the Stetson down low on his head; from beneath it, a smoky gray stare raked her face. Every muscle in his tall body rippled with displeasure. Evidently, Ben's grizzly-bear mood had continued throughout the day. This promised to be a long, long summer, Sami thought before she quietly asked, "What did you want to see me about, Mr. Woden?"

He inhaled deeply. Sami heard the sharp intake of air, watched his chest expand. His lungs held the air for a drawn-out moment before he exhaled slowly. He shook his index finger at her; his lips moved against each other, but he remained silent.

"Yes?" she prompted as his eruption developed momentum.

"Don't you 'yes' me, Sami Lassiter. I'm too mad to put up with that sassy little Arkansas tongue of yours. Watch my manners, you said. Don't curse, you said." The big finger inches from her nose shook again. "I've been watching my manners, lady. I just took those sweet little girls of yours for a horseback ride, and they both cuss like blue blazes!"

Sami suppressed a giggle. The finger jabbed again as he prompted, "Well, what do you have to say for yourself, Miss Priss?"

"I've been working with them, Mr. . . . er . . . Ben. They're just now beginning to realize the difference between certain types of words. I'll speak to them."

"Speak to them!" he repeated. "They need their little behinds paddled."

Sami had been about to smile at seeing Ben in high dudgeon, but at his words she abruptly became serious. The girls had seen enough violence to last them a lifetime. She replaced her glasses, then stared at him. "You are not to lift a finger to hurt them," she stated quietly.

His black brows soared, the rugged face stilled.

"Or . . . ?" he drawled. "You'll do what? I know what I'd like to do to you for the lectures on watching my manners when your precious little tykes' vocabulary would shame a sailor." He tipped the hat back on his dark head and stared a challenge down at her. Ben looked as deadly now as the pumas that hunted the mountain range.

Sami rounded the desk, watching the big, taut body lean toward her. She felt the hot blaze of his eyes touch her mouth, linger there. "Ah . . . I apologize for Mary Jane and Lori, Ben. I should have warned you." She eased into the big chair and slid beneath the security of the walnut desk.

Ben's eyes glittered as he watched her finger a pencil; the tension between them pounded the room. "I hate it when you look scared, Sami," he said quietly. "I wouldn't have hurt you this morning. I just wanted to touch you, to see if you were real."

To distract him, she voiced a thought that had been forming in her mind since she spoke to Mike. "Mike is very intelligent, Ben. I suspect he dropped out of school more from boredom than anything else."

"Hell, I know that." Ben sprawled in a chair and crossed his boot-shod ankles in front of him. He tossed his hat on the desk and glowered at her from under his heavy brows.

Sami felt her skin tighten as the smoky color of his eyes darkened. They drifted downward to linger over her primrose-colored blouse. She spoke as evenly as she could. "I also suspect he could use a change of friends."

Ben's hands raked his hair as he leaned his head against the back of the chair. His lids closed slowly, the hard lines settling more firmly about his mouth. One large palm swept across the planes of his face as though to erase the problem. "I agree with you. But I can't make his friends for him."

She studied the broken line of his nose and the hollows of his cheeks as the room's shadows closed in on him. "Mike's seventeenth birthday is Saturday, Ben. You might think about inviting some kids his age to a birthday party."

The black brows soared together as Ben sat upright, leaning toward her, his eyes glowering at her. "A birthday party?" he echoed, then shook his head. "You're kidding. Mike is almost a man, and he's never had a party. I'm not sure he'd even show up. And I don't know whom to invite anyway."

"You could invite some of your friends' teenage sons and daughters. It's only Wednesday; there's plenty of time to prepare."

Ben stood restlessly, shrugged his broad shoulders. "This is a ranch, lady. Not a social club."

Sami straightened from the desk. The rancher was entirely too tall, too imperiously certain of himself. "I'd like to plan a dance for Saturday night," she ventured. "With your permission, of course."

"*Here?*" The deep voice sounded incredulous.

Sami met his stare evenly. "Certainly, here. Do I have your permission?"

"You've got guts, for a teacher." The left corner of his mouth looked as if it wanted to lift into a smile, and the lines radiating from the corners of his eyes deepened. "Sure. Get together with Emma; she'll help you. I'll drive you to Lone Pine on Friday for anything you may need."

As he reached past Sami to retrieve his hat from the desk, his body neared hers, and Sami sidled away from the brush of its warmth. "Anything else, ma'am?"

"Ah . . . yes. You'll need to be here."

"Yes, ma'am." The sultry look Ben sent her from beneath his lashes sizzled the hairs on the back of her neck.

"No, ma'am." Mike shook his head and leaned back against the boards of the cattle-loading pen. He tilted his face from the dying rays of the June sun. "I'm not coming."

Sami noted how her nieces had immediately adopted Mike as Lori's hand slid about the denim covering his knee. The little girl peered up at him. On the lanky teenager's other side, Mary Jane held his hand. "Mikey, Auntie wants to give the party, and *we* get to help." She tilted her head to one side. "Are you going to spoil it, Mikey?"

Mike's petulant frown eased as he looked down at the two children. He rubbed the shiny black heads affectionately, then tugged their matching braids. "You guys don't understand."

Mary Jane's bottom lip stuck out. "I like parties, Mikey," she argued. "And Auntie said there would be dancing. Lori and me never saw dancing before."

Mike's black eyes accused Sami over the girls' heads. "I said I'd give this tutoring business a try. But a birthday party is different. We've never had any of that sissy stuff here. The guys would laugh their heads off. Besides, we had plans to have our own party down by the creek that night." He stared at her evenly. "The beer's cooling in the creek now, and Becky Westfield's getting hotter."

"You could invite your friends and Becky to the party, Mike."

He leaned against the corral and chewed on a long stem of grass. "They're not the kind of guys Dad likes. And we've never had a party here for as long as I can remember. What does *he* think of this harebrained idea, anyway?"

Lori and Mary Jane climbed the rails to perch beside Mike's shoulder. He watched their slow progress intently, then carefully secured the back straps of their bib overalls in his hands.

"Auntie is baking a big cake for the party." Lori's small hands moved expansively, indicating the cake's size. "She's putting candles all over the top. And there's gonna be ice cream and dancing—"

"Nope. I wouldn't be caught dead at a bash like that. Sorry, girls." He looked down at Sami. "It's going to be worth all this book crap just to see you sweat it out, teach. You'll be sorry you didn't take my offer. Forget the party. Hey!" He edged from the probe of a tiny finger in the coils of his ear. "Watch it, Lori."

"Auntie wants a party. So do I. So do Mary Jane and Emma, too," Lori stated stubbornly. "You and your Dad are sourpusses."

Sami interrupted to correct her. "Mike's father wants this party, Lori. He's even taking us to Lone Pine shopping Friday morning."

"You've got to be kidding." Mike scutinized Sami's face. "Dad really agreed to this? He always says that stuff is bunk."

"Um-hmm." Behind her back, Sami crossed her fingers.

Mike lifted the girls by their overall backstraps and placed them safely on the ground. "Count me out. I've got to clean out the horses' stalls. See you later."

He looked over her head. "Staying kind of close to the ranch, aren't you, Dad? I've got to hand it to you, she's got more nerve than I thought she'd have."

"Hi, Benjamin," Mary Jane greeted Ben. "Can we ride old Ornery Cuss now?"

"'Benjamin'?" Sami repeated as she turned to face him. The name was pleasant as it crossed her tongue. Also pleasant was Ben's look of discomfort. He reminded her of a small boy caught with his hand deep in the cookie jar. The petulant jut of his jaw hardened. His eyes glittered as Sami heard Mike's first chuckle.

"Emma calls Dad 'Benjamin.' See you guys later." Mike tugged the girls' braids again and faced Sami. "I meant what I said, teach. Count me out."

"Wait for us, Mikey. We want to watch you pile the

horse"—Mary Jane glanced slyly at her aunt—"stuff," she finished lamely before running after Lori and Mike.

Ben watched his son's rawboned frame saunter toward the huge red barn before his eyes shifted back to coldly dissect Sami's smile. "Okay, teach," he said, using Mike's name for her, "are you beginning to get the picture?"

She avoided looking at him, sought the serenity of the snowcapped mountains beyond Ben's rawly masculine stance. "I see two bachelors, each hardheaded and each set in his ways . . . Benjamin," she added for good measure.

He stripped the leather gloves from his hands and jammed them into his belt. "Just what do you mean by that remark, lady?" he asked with deadly intent. "I was married twice, you know. Mike's too young to be set in his ways. And I'm not all that old."

Sami took a deep breath and leveled her next sentence at him. "Mike acts as if he doesn't need to make any concessions to other people's feelings. You project the same attitude. A certificate of learning isn't the only thing your son needs, Mr. Woden. He needs an example of humanity."

Darkly, Ben's expression homed in on her upturned face. "I see. Your lunatic party idea failed, and you want to take it out on me. Well, be careful, ma'am," he warned. "I *do* have feelings, and you might not want to take the consequences if I get riled." His gaze stripped her of her prim blouse and skirt and left her standing in her panties. Sami crossed her arms over her breasts to protect them from his heated stare.

"Don't rile me, ma'am." The sound of his growl filtered through her clothing, penetrating her flesh. "Mike and I got along okay before you came. We can do okay after you leave."

"At least Mike's promised to give the GED a chance, Mr. Woden. Now it's your turn to give *him* a chance."

"Oh?" The arch of a single black brow taunted her.

"Now you're going to tell me how to be a good father?" He tilted the battered hat back on his head, his weight braced against the length of one leg. "Full speed ahead, right?"

Sami didn't want to feel the anger that began to curl her fingers into her palms. The small flicker at the corner of his hard mouth mocked her.

"You're quite a package," he remarked amiably as she fought to control her rage. "Quite a female."

His cocksure attitude grated on Sami's strained temper, and she erupted. "Your assessment of me is as welcome as fleas on a dog!"

Ben reached out and lifted her glasses off her face, then tucked them inside his breast pocket and grinned down at her. "I'm open for negotiations, ma'am."

Sami took a deep, steadying breath, trying to unknot her fists as she strove to meet the sensual warmth of his stare. "Ma'am?" he prompted lazily. Sami eyed the biceps straining at the faded cloth, the obviously light places in the worn denim jeans across his hips and down his legs. She thought of herself as a tightly restrained woman, but Ben raised instincts within her that were hard to control. Uncomfortable instincts. Exactly how did one negotiate with a cowboy?

"Very well," she said coolly. "Mike can easily pass his GED. He's agreed to study. But I think he needs more than the scholastic side of education."

Ben's boots settled deeper in the dust. "Like what?"

"Well . . ." Sami saw his amusement fade, watched the spark of interest grow in his eyes. "He needs to learn social skills as well as academic subjects. I think the idea of giving him a birthday party is a good one. It's a start, anyway. We can take it one step at a time after that."

"Mmm." His hand chafed the hardness of his jaw, then rummaged through the thick hair tufting on his chest. Sami fought against the sudden urge to run her fingers through that roughness. She felt a hollowness in her lower stomach, and her mouth was dry. Her eyes followed his hand as it returned to tug his hat down over his forehead. "Mike won't be there," he said. "What do you recommend?"

Sami's tension eased. Benjamin Woden might disconcert her, but there was no doubting his sincerity about his son. "Will *you* be there, Ben?"

"Hell, what kind of a father do you think I am? You plan the damn thing; I'll be there. Just make a list of the things you need, and I'll get them for you." He kicked the powder-dry dirt once and added, "I'll take the girls while you're working on the party, if you don't mind. Just to get them out of your hair."

Early Saturday evening, Emma nudged Sami's side as she carried Mike's cake into the huge living room, weaving her way among the noisy partygoers. "Yellow is a pretty color on dark-haired people, Sami. I like that skirt and blouse; you look real nice." She carefully placed the candle-decked chocolate cake on the table and smiled at Sami. "See Lori and Mary Jane peeping down here from the stairway? They just may sit there all night."

Emma glanced at Ben, who was lounging against a paneled wall. "Oh, Benjamin might grumble, but he's slickered up, Sami. He's a fine cut of a man in that red dress shirt and those dark slacks. And Mike's been ornery as a coyote, but I saw the way his eyes lit up when Judy Thacker walked into this house," she murmured. "All that horseplay while the kids were eating pizza was for her benefit, I betcha."

"Huh. There must be twenty kids here, woman. Too much noise, too much commotion," Dan muttered as he carried in two more liters of soft drinks and a fresh bowl of ice. "Look what they're doing now."

Quickly, the teenagers moved the furniture back against the walls, rolled up the rugs, and tossed them into the corners. The stairway light spread across the bare boards of the living-room floor as they began a lively dance to the loud music coming from Mike's stereo.

"Come on, Emma," Dan grumbled. "You've been cooking and cleaning all day for this shindig. I'm tired. Let's go on home."

"Misery loves company, Dan. Stay awhile." Ben joined them, lifted his glass of cola, and stared at it. "This needs a little something. How about it, Dan? We can hole up in my study." He glanced darkly down at Sami before tipping his glass to his lips and muttering, "That's been the only safe place during all this confusion. I just hope it's worth all the trouble."

Sami, riding on the tide of her success, disregarded his complaint as she watched Judy Thacker approach Mike and tug him to the makeshift dance floor. Mike's eyes darted toward Sami, and she winked back at him. "Do you have any slower tapes, Carol?" she asked the blond girl in charge of the music. Moments later, Mike's arms latched about Judy, and he grinned over at Sami.

"Now, that's worth all this commotion, Benjamin," Emma breathed softly. "Judy's a whole sight better than the company Mike's been keeping lately. She comes from good people, she does. You can manage now, I guess. I'm taking my tired old man here and going to the cabin. Real nice party, Sami. See you in the morning."

"It *is* a nice party, Sami," Ben admitted as he set his cola on the table. "I just realized that Mike likes the Thacker girl. So I guess all the time and preparations were worthwhile. He's a happy kid right now." He glanced down at her. "You've got a pretty smile on your face, ma'am. Pleased with yourself?"

"Immensely. Aren't you proud of Mike?"

"I've always been proud of him. It's just that we go toe-to-toe about almost everything." He was silent a moment as he watched the teenagers, then said, "We're receiving some get-lost looks, ma'am. Would you like to step out on the front porch?"

"I would, Mr. Woden."

Outside, Sami stood watching the stars, her hands braced against the railing. It was the first week of June, and the evening air was fresh and cool. "It's a wonderful night."

Aware of his silence, she turned to face Ben and found herself looking up into his face. "Dance, ma'am?" he asked softly. Without waiting for her reply, his strong arms encircled her to draw her to him.

"Yes, I'd like that," Sami agreed as she tried to wedge some distance between them, her palms against his chest. But his hand cupped the back of her head and held it to him as he slowly moved to the music coming from inside the house.

His fingers lifted her face to his. "I don't feel much different from my son right now, lady. But there's a big difference between him and me. A lot of years and a lot of experience." The moon caught the glitter of his eyes. "And there's a whole lot of difference between you and me, isn't there?"

Uncomfortable with his intensity, Sami was silent. She felt safer when he angered her. Quickly, she changed the subject. "I want to thank you for being so patient with Mary Jane and Lori, Mr. Woden. It's really nice of you to teach them how to ride—"

"I'm not talking about Mike or your girls," he interrupted savagely. "You know what I mean. I'm talking about the difference between you and me. Education, manners . . . years," he ended bitterly. "Damn it, don't go all wide-eyed and scared. I wouldn't hurt you. But in the week you've been here, you've gotten to me, lady. I smell your powder in the bathroom and I remember how you looked that first morning here. I wanted to strip that godawful robe from you and carry you to my bed. I want to now. See?" he accused as he released her.

"You're so wrapped up in books that you go white if a man looks at you as a woman."

"I'm here to teach Mike, Mr. Woden. Your problems are your own."

"You are my problem right now. Do you realize you flinch every time I come near you? You skitter around me as if I were the one who hurt you. The kids trust me; why can't you?" His voice softened to the sexy baritone Sami knew was more dangerous than his grizzly-bear mood in the mornings. The rough pad of his thumb caressed the satiny texture of her cheek, swept across it before he muttered, "I'd like to meet the bastard who made you man-shy, little bit."

She didn't want to pursue the subject with him. "Well, let's just say that I've seen the unpleasant side of a man."

"What about your husband? Was your marriage good?" he asked.

"Ben . . ." she warned. Did he have to pry at her memories?

"I wonder," he murmured. "For a widow woman, you seem almost virginal."

She found no ridicule in his face, only a piercing curiosity. Perhaps it was the success of the party or the sweetness of the pine-scented evening breeze, but a need for companionship lurked about big, tough Ben Woden, and Sami could find no offense in his remark. "Des was a beautiful person. Sensitive and kind. He was the best thing in my life."

. . . And she loved him, Ben finished mentally. From the moment he'd seen Sami Lassiter, he'd wanted to love her, to protect her even from his own desires. That was the reason he'd stopped their lovemaking at her trailer.

"We enjoyed the same things," Sami murmured. "Art, books, music."

"He was a lucky man." Those things had never been a part of his life, Ben mused, oddly uncomfortable with

Sami's past and her soft, whimsical smile. Damn. None of his emotions for this petite woman were gentle. They were fierce, consuming. Right now, he wanted to kiss her, to open the yellow pearl buttons of her blouse and taste the enticing sweetness beneath. Lord, how he wanted to do those two things . . . and much, much more.

- 5 -

TWO WEEKS AFTER the party, Sami stood beside Mike at a window in the study, watching Ben lead an old horse named Ornery Cuss around the perimeter of the corral. On the horse's back, Mary Jane clung tightly to Lori's waist, and Lori gripped the saddle horn with both hands. Dressed in their everyday bib overalls, Sami's nieces giggled, their braids bouncing up and down. Chug, the huge Saint Bernard, plodded at Ben's heels.

"Dad used to do that for me once in a while, when I was a kid," Mike said wistfully. "He's been doing it every morning with the girls while we're in class. We're in here cracking the books, and they're outside having a ball."

"Sometimes I think it's a lot safer with him out there and us in here," Sami said thoughtfully. "He has his rough moments."

Companionably, Mike nudged her with his elbow. "Dad may be grouchy with everyone else, but I've noticed the kids crawl up on his lap every chance they get.

They helped Emma bake brownies the other day for a secret picnic with him. It's funny, but I never thought of Dad spending much time with little kids. He was always so busy when I was growing up."

Outside the window, Ben lifted his hat from his head. He tapped it on Ornery Cuss's sunken flanks. The old horse tried a few trots, then returned to his plodding. Ben grinned up at the girls' giggles, and beneath her folded arms, Sami's heart began to thump unevenly. In the last week, Ben had avoided her as though she were Typhoid Mary; he actually recoiled when she came near him.

His warmth still clung to the huge study chair in the mornings, and Sami found herself snuggling to it and inhaling his masculine scent. The last few days, he'd breakfasted and left the house before the rest of the household even arose. He had returned promptly at five-thirty in the evening, showered and changed and sat down at the dinner table at six o'clock for Emma's evening meal. As they ate, his scant conversation seemed to deliberately exclude Sami, and his flickering glances at her lacked warmth. After dinner, he spent the remainder of the evening in the study.

"It's nice having you here, Sami," Mike stated quietly behind her.

Reluctantly, Sami forced her eyes from the window and the blaze of Ben's smile. She hadn't meant her wistful sigh to be heard, but the brightness in Mike's black eyes acknowledged it.

"Dad may act like a varmint toward you, Sami, but the time you and the girls have spent here is the nicest time in my life." Mike tried his compliments uncertainly now, weighed her reaction to them, and beamed with his success.

"That's very nice of you to say, Mike. Thank you."

"Yeah, well. Somebody has to say it. The house seems more like a home now, even with Dad acting like a sorehead. I think he kind of likes having you and the girls here, too, despite the looks I've seen him give you."

Sami couldn't stop herself from asking, "What looks?"

Mike's eyebrows lifted. "Like a starved dog looks at a bone," he replied bluntly. Sami waited eagerly for him to elaborate, but instead he changed the subject. "Hey, how do you think I'm coming with the GED stuff?"

"You're doing fine, Mike. I think I'm going to win my bet with you."

Mike pushed a book aside to sit on the desk. "I want to learn to paint, Sami. Get me started, will you?"

Sami was surprised and pleased at his interest in art. "We could include painting in your afternoon lessons, and you can come with me to the mountains to paint on weekends, too, if you'd like."

"That's great. I never thought I'd be into art, but you're making changes around here, Sami. And I like it."

She smiled and said to him teasingly, "Changes? You must be talking about the computer your father bought for you as an educational tool. *You* conned me into presenting the idea to him. I bet he doesn't know a thing about the enormous number of games you've ordered."

"Hey!" Mike's expression was indignant. "Would I buy games?" When she laughed, he added softly, "Really, it's nice here now, Sami. Dad's got more people to fight with, so it sort of takes the pressure off me. He even asked me to play poker with him last night." He looked directly at her. "He's having another bathroom put in upstairs."

Sami remembered her encounter with Ben outside the bathroom that first morning. "I suppose he wants his privacy."

"Could be. But I got the impression he just wanted to do something nice for you." Mike leaned against the desk as he studied her. "Judy is a lady, too, teach," he observed slowly. "She makes me nervous. I keep worrying that I'm going to say the wrong thing. I kind of think Dad's got the same problem with you. Women are different; you never know how things will hit 'em."

"Judy is lovely, Mike."

"Yep," he agreed. "I've got major plans in that direction. She thinks I need a haircut. What do you think?"

Sami studied his angular bones and raven hair. "Is that why you've been spending so much time in the bathroom? I think a new hairstyle would be just the thing, Mike."

"Good. You said I'm way ahead of your study schedule, so I made an appointment with a barber in Lone Pine for this afternoon. Then I thought I'd sort of drop by Judy's house later. I could take Lori and Mary Jane to see the Thackers' new kittens. What do you think?"

"Now I *know* you're a con artist, Mike." Sami laughed. "You set me up for that one. And I know taking the girls to see the kittens is just an excuse for you to see Judy. But you're right; you are doing very well, and I agree that you're due for a break." She winked. "Stop in the dry goods store while you're in town, Mike. You could use some new jeans and shirts."

"Yeah?" Mike scanned the worn leather of his boots. "What about boots, too?"

Before she could answer, Mike's head turned toward the sound of footsteps beyond the study door. "That's Dad. Hey, Dad!" he called. "Come here."

The footsteps slowed in the hallway, and Ben opened the door with his left hand. Lori and Mary Jane gripped his right hand. He glanced at Sami, then at his son. The rugged planes of his face seemed to change from pleasure to wariness. "Did you call me, Mike?"

Lori stepped in front of Ben's long legs and crossed her arms petulantly. "We're on a secret mission, Mikey. Benjamin's our leader."

Mike snorted, then slid off the desk to cross the room to her. He tossed her up in the air, then caught her in his arms and grinned at his father. "We've already had two secret raids on Emma's chocolate chip cookies this morning, Dad. Did you get snared into making another one?"

Ben leaned down to lift Mary Jane into his arms. "This is the second mission for me, too. They were jumping on my bed before anyone else was awake."

"Good morning, Ben," Sami spoke quietly at Mike's side. "I'm sorry the children disturbed you."

Her normally soft voice contained a husky inflection that caught Ben's attention. He stared at her, and the other people in the room seemed to vanish. "It's all right," he heard himself say. "I was ready to get up anyway."

He felt his throat tighten, and her name formed on his lips. "Sami."

At that moment, Ben Wade Woden wished for the impossible: that the beautiful woman and *all* the children in the room were his.

The midmorning light, crossing into the room from the window, outlined Sami's petite body. Her full curves, beneath the lacy blue blouse and gathered skirt, stopped Ben's breath. He forced himself to swallow as he sought her face in the shadows of the room. He needed to see behind her oversized glasses to her eyes. He knew they were like a doe's, soft and dark.

Her mouth could make a man lose his mind. It could be as soft and timid beneath his . . . her lips could search his hungrily, untutored, but with all the passion of a woman. His stomach contracted as a sensual warmth began to curl through his loins. He shifted the child in his arms to conceal the rising thrust of his desire.

Damn. He'd give his soul to have Sami in his bed. No, not just in his bed, he admitted, in his life. He needed her softness, wanted to erase her fears, to take on his larger shoulders her problems. He let the breath seep slowly from his lungs as he acknowledged Sami

Lassiter's impact on his life. She had changed it as a rock slide changes the contours of a mountain.

"Hey, Dad," Mike spoke softly at his side. "How about letting me have the Bronco this afternoon? Sami says I'm ahead of her study schedule and it's okay to take a break."

Reluctantly, Ben forced his gaze to his son. "What?"

"May I borrow the Bronco?" Mike repeated. "I've got some stuff to do in town, and I thought I'd take the girls over to see the Thackers' new kittens. It's all right with Sami. Emma wants some groceries, and I can pick up some of that plumbing stuff for you. How about it?"

Ben noted the eagerness in his son's expression. "Seeing Judy isn't on your list, is it, Mike?"

Mike's stance shifted to defensiveness immediately. "Something wrong with that?" he asked edgily.

When had things changed between his son and himself? Ben wondered. When had the banter become bickering? A long time ago, he answered himself silently. But Sami and the girls had changed Mike again: He laughed now.

"I didn't say there was anything wrong with it," Ben answered quietly. "But while you're in town, stop by the telephone company and see about getting a phone of your own. That way you can talk to Judy any time you want without disturbing my business calls."

"You mean it, Dad?" Mike's question held amazement. "All right!"

His son's enthusiasm suddenly made Ben feel the lonely weight of his years. It settled heavily about his shoulders, ached in every scar he'd gained on the rodeo circuit. Lord, how he wanted Sami's warmth.

He watched her cross the room and smile down at her nieces. Within him, the pain grew more intense; when it was knife-sharp in intensity, he could stand it no longer.

"Here." He shoved Lori into Mike's free arm. "See me before you go. I'll get a list of things ready." A searing pain ripped through him as he closed the oak door behind him.

Sami raised her knuckles to the study door, then stopped to listen to the silence that had lasted throughout the afternoon. It was eight o'clock; Emma and Dan had retired to their home, yet silence thundered ominously from behind the closed door of the study. She took a deep breath, swallowed, balanced the dinner tray on her left hand, and knocked with her right.

The heavy oak did not muffle the roar of Ben's deep voice. "Leave me alone," he ordered.

Sami closed her eyes, remembering Ben's rugged face as it had appeared during this morning's encounter. His expression had been one of longing and pain. Taking a deep breath, she whispered. "Ben Woden, if you've got a bottle in front of you, you're on your own."

When she opened the door, Ben roared from the darkness, "What the hell do you want? Can't a man have any peace around here anymore?"

The smell of whiskey permeated the room, but as Sami's eyes adjusted to the darkness, she saw that the bottle was still almost full.

"Good evening, Ben." She spoke with a softness she didn't feel as she placed the tray on the desk beside the bottle. "Getting ready to tie one on, are you?"

The old rage at seeing a man about to drink heavily grew within Sami, slightly surprising her. She had thought she was over that now, but the tremor of anger rippling through her indicated otherwise. Her fingers trembled as she unwrapped the turkey sandwich and poured two cups of hot tea.

Ben's big hand wrapped itself about the whiskey bottle, and he lifted it to his lips. He drank, grimaced, and replaced the bottle on the desk. "Hell, yes. I'll tie one on if I want to." The fierce brows lowered over his pewter-colored eyes when Sami turned on the desk lamp. "Leave that thing off!"

Sami calmly placed a cup of tea before him, sat down, and began to sip her own. "Did I ever tell you that you remind me of a grizzly bear, Ben?"

"I don't want you here, woman. Get out!"

"I won't get out tonight, Ben," Sami murmured with a lightness she didn't feel. "Mike called from town to say Judy's horse is foaling. He's sleeping at the Thackers' tonight, and the girls are staying with Eileen. They'll all be home in the morning, so there's nothing to worry about. Have some tea. It's a delicious blend."

Bathed by the lamp's dim light, Ben's expression was savage. His lips were tightly clenched, and the break in his nose seemed more pronounced. "Why are you here? I'm sure it's not because it's tea time in the Rockies."

He stared at her hair. "Where's the bun? That tight little topknot goes with those touch-me-not clothes you wear like a suit of armor." He raked his eyes over her lavender sweater and worn jeans. "Dressed like that, you look almost old enough for a training bra."

Sami knew his own inner hurt was causing him to lash out at her. "That's it, Ben," she invited softly. "Say anything you want. Get it off your chest. I'd rather you talk than drink."

He stared at her. "I drink many nights," he admitted baldly. "It helps me sleep."

"Not tonight, Ben."

"Really, little bit?" he drawled. "What else have you planned?" The sensuous rumbling of his voice stroked the fine hairs on the nape of Sami's neck.

"Mmm, we could talk. At least until whatever is eating you eases." Right now she needed Ben's companionship as much as he needed hers. Sami wanted to hear his voice, hear the Wyoming cowboy drawl softly into the lonesome night. Wary, belligerent, and tough, Ben needed her. And for tonight, she liked the feeling of being needed by a man.

"The coyotes are howling outside," she began conversationally. "Do you realize I've been here just under three weeks and I've seen little of your ranch, other than a few glimpses on short walks with Mary Jane and Lori?"

Ben's hard lips pressed against each other for what seemed a century, and his smoke-gray eyes narrowed at her. "You've got nerve, little bit. Big nerve for a small lady," he added with a rueful smile. "You're alone in this house with a man twice your size, a man who's knocked around this big world a lot more than you have. I'm hurting now, but inside me there's a voice saying you could make everything come out right tonight."

Despite the coolness of the study, the blood in Sami's veins grew warm. Her mouth felt suddenly dry.

Ben desired her; his smoke-colored eyes asked the question his lips would not. Sami trembled, and the hot tea sloshed over the rim of the cup, scalding her skin. She rubbed the back of her hand slowly.

She closed her eyes, and the image of Ben making love to her appeared behind her lids. Sami felt his urgency across the room, felt it lock into the bones of her body and coil primitively about her abdomen. She opened her eyes but kept them lowered to avoid the heat of his gaze as she said aloud, "That wouldn't solve anything, Ben. For either one of us."

"Then we'd better get out of this house, lady. Because I want you like hell. Enough to carry you up those stairs." In a lithe motion, Ben rose and stalked toward her, his boots echoing on the hardwood floor. When he stood over her, Sami turned her face up, sensing the harshness of his expression even before she saw it. The planes of his face were etched with torment, and the cords of his sinewy neck seemed to tighten. "Sami?" he asked.

Sami didn't want to touch the callused palm that stretched out to her. She didn't want the smoothness of her flesh to slide over it, or the strength of his large fingers to ease between the slenderness of her own. Yet, somehow, his big hand held hers, and she couldn't make herself pull free. Mesmerized by the intensity of his expression, she allowed him to draw her to her feet, allowed him to take the teacup from her hand and place it on the table.

"Come with me." Low and husky, his voice was tremulous; his rugged face was uncertain.

"Yes." Her single word startled her. For so long, she had succeeded in protecting the emotions that could make her susceptible to a man. But in the loneliness of the night, Ben had reached out to her, and, as a woman and a friend, she had instinctively responded to his need. Within her mind, Sami had the odd sensation of closing the door on old memories and stepping into the future as she met his eyes.

His free hand rose to her face. The heat from his open palm grazed her skin. "Sami," he murmured softly. "So small. So feminine." The big hand shook slightly as a callused fingertip stroked the length of her cheek. "Come with me, Sami."

Outside, the June night was damp and fragrant, scented with lodgepole pine. Limousin and Hereford cattle grazed on the moon-kissed fescue fields as Sami stood outside the ranch barn draped in Ben's denim jacket.

She smoothed the worn fabric with the flat of her hand, tucked her nose down into the worn collar. It bore Ben's scent, and she thought of how he had wrapped it about her gently. He had adjusted the collar with shaking hands, then lifted the long sweep of her hair to arrange it carefully about her shoulders. His expression had been tender, the warmth in his eyes reflected in the pleased curve of his lips. "I won't hurt you," he had murmured.

"I know," she had responded. Now she gripped the large jacket as it began to slide off her shoulders. Ben could raise her temper as no other man had, and yet he could extract a surprising tenderness from her.

A feeling of uncertainty stirred within her, and her face grew taut as she frowned. For years, she had denied her own physical and emotional needs, fearing the pain that would result from the loss of another love. She was only sharing a few empty hours with Ben, not making a lifetime commitment, but he threatened to peel back her emotional scar tissue by exposing his soul. As a companion and as a lover, she knew she could meet his needs for the night. But at what cost to herself? Was she on the brink of falling in love again?

Slow hoofbeats sounded within the barn, then grew louder. Ben shouldered aside the huge door as he led Revenge, his Appaloosa stallion, through it. One hand resting on the horse's black mane, he said, "Sami?"

She lifted her head to stare up at him. His voice caused a shimmering inside her, a feeling of danger. The husky timbre seemed like that of lone wolf calling his mate. *His mate*. Sami felt a small shiver of misgiving. Would he want too much?

Beneath the light of the full moon, she knew Ben read the stark emotions racing across her face as she saw the taut bitterness return to the planes of his. Her grief for Des had just healed. She'd loved him deeply, trusted him, and revealed her secret agonies to him.

Ben's large body loomed before her; the moonlight was silvery on his tousled hair. The light bathed the wide expanse of his shoulders and the long spread of his muscled legs. He was primitive and exciting, yet Sami was not ready for the emotions he raked from within her. She *could* love him—beyond the blazing sensuality he evoked in her. The possibility of loving Ben stunned, then frightened her.

Tension ached in her throat as she took a step backward. Above her, Ben's face was starkly lighted, his eyebrows a single, fierce line. "Ben, I . . ."

"You've changed your mind," he finished in a cold clip of words. The Appaloosa snorted, sensing the humans' tension; his huge hooves pawed the ground.

"Easy, boy." Ben's free hand stroked the horse's neck. "Settle down." His eyes flicked down the length of Sami's body.

The arrogant tilt of his head and the stance of his long legs challenged Sami. Ben wouldn't understand her doubts, she thought. She sensed his condemnation and straightened her backbone against it before he spoke. "You're afraid. And no proper lady would take a moonlight ride with an old cowboy like me, would she?"

Sami stared at him. Somehow, Ben had misconstrued her natural hesitation to enter into a deeper relationship with him. In the moments when she had been examining her innermost fears, her past and her future, he had evidently decided she was a snob. And a frightened one, at that. The tension she had been experiencing moments before and Ben's slightly contemptuous tone did not mix together well. In an effort to control her lurching emotions, Sami swallowed and gripped his jacket tightly around her.

But against her better judgment, anger began to curl inside her stomach. He *did* have the ability to punch all the wrong buttons, and he knew exactly how to misread her. "I am not frightened. Where's my horse?" Sami stated as evenly as she could, rising to his challenge despite her caution.

"Revenge can carry both of us," Ben said curtly. "Are you coming?"

"How do I get up?" She glimpsed his smile just before his hands spanned her waist to lift her. He placed her on Revenge, then swung up behind her. Controlling the stallion with his fingers, he circled her waist with his right arm.

Despite her wariness, Sami pressed her back into the safety of Ben's chest as the big horse sidestepped briskly. Ben's breath brushed her cheek as she gripped his forearm with both hands. He chuckled. "Easy, woman. Revenge wants to run. He'd like to show off for you."

As if to verify his statement, the stallion snorted and tossed his head. Beneath Sami's clutching fingers, Ben's corded arm tightened as he easily controlled the stallion.

Braced by the strength of Ben's body, Sami saw the moonlit ground. It seemed two miles down. "Ah . . . Ben?"

He lifted a strand of her long hair that had been caught between their bodies. Slipping his hand across Sami's chest, he held her upper left arm, drawing her back against him. Sami gripped his forearm with every ounce of strength she possessed. "Ben," she began again as a dry wad of fear slipped down her throat. "I don't think—"

"Shush, little bit," he whispered in her ear. "Lean back. Relax. If you don't stop shaking so hard, Revenge will want to run instead of walk." He placed his head alongside hers. "Shush, now. I'll take care of you." He clicked his tongue and pressed his thighs into Revenge's sides, urging the horse forward.

As they rode into the night, the Appaloosa's slow gait settled Sami deeper into the cradle of Ben's body. Gradually, enfolded by his strength, she relaxed. The slow, swaying rhythm of the horse soothed her, silent contentment slipping over her as lightly as the evening dew.

With a tired sigh, Sami welcomed the solace. Her thoughtful mood before the ride slipped back upon her. She hadn't allowed herself to depend on anyone else since Des died. But tonight, she trusted Ben, shared the camaraderie of loneliness with him. A feeling of security settled warmly within her.

The heavy weight of his arm slid down to wrap about her waist, his fingers pressed into the soft indentation. The only sounds in the stillness of the moonlight were the steady hoofbeats of the horse. A long time later, Sami gave an involuntary, wistful sigh.

Ben leaned down to whisper into her ear, "What are you thinking, little bit?" Guiding the horse with the pressure of his knees and the strength of his hand, Ben loved the soft feel of the woman within the circle of his arm. He'd ached for her ever since she'd come to his ranch. It had been torture for him to listen to her lilting voice; enticing as a southern breeze, it tormented him until he could not sleep. Now, her small shoulders fitted to the hardness of his chest, the softness of her buttocks seemed to snuggle into him . . .

He eased his fingers deeper into the small indentation at her waist. Lord, she was soft. A loving woman scarred deeply by some bastard.

He'd never moved to the crook of a woman's finger, but when Sami had set her tiny foot down tonight in the study, forcing him to share his emptiness, the earth seemed to go all cockeyed for him. Sami had allowed a little of the curtain surrounding her to lift, and he wanted to know more about her. He smoothed the denim covering her waist and allowed his chin to settle on the sleek, fragrant mass of her hair.

His lips moved in the dark tresses to form a small smile. Sami Lassiter's silky Arkie drawl belied her spunk, but she'd shown her true colors tonight. She'd wanted him away from his bottle, and so had pried him from it and used herself to do it. Revenge must have looked like an elephant to her. He'd read the fright in her face, felt it in her rigid body.

She was quiet now, learning to match her body movements to the horse's rhythm. Ben guided the Appaloosa toward a knoll overlooking his ranch and repeated his question. "What are you thinking?"

Her laughter sounded like music, weakening Ben's

determination not to slip his other hand around her. Gently, naturally, it settled on the slenderness of her thigh as Revenge continued to follow the old trail.

Sami stirred in his arms. "I'm thinking that Revenge is a lot bigger than an Arkansas mule, and I'm likely to be quite sore in the morning."

Ben nuzzled the spot where her neck and shoulder joined, amazed that she still leaned against him. "What would you know about mules, lady?"

His heart did flip-flops when she giggled. "You'd be surprised. Dory, our mule, was the only transportation between the Arkansas hills and the grocery store. Sitting on her sharp backbone felt a lot better than walking over rocks when we didn't have shoes. And Dory could haul more bags of poke greens and sassafras root than my sister and I could carry in ten trips."

He smiled again, pleased that Sami had shared a portion of her past with him. He wanted to know everything about her.

The Appaloosa slowed to a halt at the end of the trail, and though Ben felt he could hold Sami forever, she shifted uncomfortably in his arms. Reluctantly, he released her and slid back over Revenge's rump to the ground. He lifted his arms for Sami.

"Come on down, little bit." He saw her indecision, then slowly, light as a butterfly, her smooth hands met his callused ones. "Revenge can graze while we talk."

His eyes almost closed with the pleasure of her touch as her hands glided to his shoulders and rested there. His hands slid down to span her small waist. He couldn't help pulling her against the length of his body, couldn't help lowering her softness slowly down his hardness until her toes met the ground. There was something in her eyes tonight that matched his loneliness.

"Tell me about Dory," he urged as he laced his fingers with hers and guided her to a rock shelf. He dusted the ledge with the flat of his hand and swept his palm toward it. "Best seats in the house, lady."

She laughed for the second time that night, and an emotion as powerful as his will to live surged through Ben. The very sound made him want to laugh with her. Tonight, he felt as if he could ride the meanest side-winder bronc on the rodeo circuit. It was a feeling he hadn't had since his youth. It was a feeling he wanted to have when he was eighty, and he wanted the woman causing it, wanted her *now*.

Ben hadn't realized he was gazing down at her until she asked, "Why are you staring at me, Mr. Benjamin Woden?" The gentleness of her voice caused him to reel, as if he were being drawn into the very softness of her. When she looked up at him closely, Ben spread his legs farther apart and locked his knees to keep his balance.

Sami carefully examined the craggy planes of his face and the masculine stance blending with the primitive peaks of the Rocky Mountains behind him. The evening breeze swished the pine branches above them, and she felt a cold chill run down to her toes. The tilt of his head, the shadows sweeping his face, and the jut of his broken nose bore the intensity of a hunter sighting in on his prey. He allowed Sami's fingers to slip from his as she sat on the flat rock.

His eyes drifted over the length of her body slowly, and protectively, Sami drew her knees up, wrapping her arms about her shins. She rested her chin on her knees and stared at the valley below. Ben wanted her, she thought. He stalked her too closely, reached in and twisted her good intentions apart. She didn't want him scraping her emotions raw. It had taken her years to reach the measure of peace she'd attained before she met him.

"It's a beautiful night," she remarked quietly to counter the wild conflict within her.

"Yep."

Revenge chomped steadily on the range grass, the coyotes howled somewhere in the darkness, and Sami's heart thumped against her chest as Ben stared steadily down at her.

"'Yep.' Standard western lingo, cowboy?" she teased. She liked the gravelly sound of his chuckle and wanted to hear it again.

"Yep. How's your pretty little bottom feeling?" Ben's husky statement was all male invitation, enhanced by the flash of white teeth in his shadowed face. "Want me to rub it?"

The thought of his callused palm touching her there raised goose bumps on Sami's flesh. She shivered, then shifted uneasily on the rock. "You're out of line, Ben."

"Not for what I have planned, ma'am. I've just decided it's open season on schoolmarms, little bit."

His softly spoken words dropped down to her through the pine-scented night air with all the deadly intent of a hunter's bullets. "You're a helluva loving woman beneath those prim manners. I intend to make love with you so hard you'll never look at another man. You're going to be mine right down to the dimple in your chin."

When Ben propped a booted foot on the ledge beside her, Sami's breath caught in her throat. He circled her nerveless fingers with the heat of his strong ones and drew the back of her hand to his mouth. He nibbled her knuckles gently, sending electric shocks up her arm.

Over their joined hands, he whispered, "Don't look so astounded, Sami. You've brought more enjoyment and excitement into my life than I've ever known. Your kindness and your gentleness touch everyone around you. Even Chug's enchanted. I'd be a fool to let you escape."

Sami ran the tip of her tongue over her suddenly dry bottom lip. Her heart thudded heavily against the confines of her chest. "We, uh, we'd better go back to the ranch."

His chuckle vibrated in the forest's stillness. "I thought you'd take it like that, honey." He turned her palms upward, grazed them with the fine edges of his teeth. "Sweet," he stated. "Yet just ornery enough to make the hunting worthwhile."

Sami tried to draw her hand away from his fiery mouth, but could not. She tried again, her fingers slipping from his warm clasp. Ben caused those fluttery emotions to rise in the pit of her stomach. He also caused the weakness in her legs, the melting warmth growing deep in the most feminine places in her body. Part of her wanted to seek the shelter of his arms, while all the remaining parts wanted to run from the danger he represented.

"I'm a tutor for Mike, nothing more . . ." she began shakily. *Why did he have to look so sexy?* She'd avoided other possible entanglements with no regrets. *Why did she want to snuggle in those strong arms?* It was a ridiculous situation, she decided. Both of them were too old and too different from each other to even think . . .

"You're more than a tutor, Sami. Mike's laughing now for the first time since he was a child. Everyone around you feels your loving ways. Don't you think you could spare a little of that for me?" The need stamped in his tone and the ache etched in his rugged face sent Sami's intentions spinning sideways.

"I . . . I'd really like to go back now," she said. Her insides churned; her legs were as wobbly as a toddler's. She badly wanted the safety of other people, the distraction of Mike's problems, and the antics of the girls.

"Okay," he agreed slowly. "But remember what I said, Sami. As far as I'm concerned, it's open season on pretty little brown-eyed teachers."

In the next few days, Sami found it impossible to avoid Ben's alert gaze. His eyes caught hers, leaving her breathless. His slow, knowing grin completely disarmed her.

For the space of a few hours each day, Sami avoided

Ben's pursuit. After the last afternoon class, she and Mike packed their painting supplies into the Bronco. The majestic purple and blue Rockies acted as a balm to Sami's unsettled emotions. Concentrating on her own painting and teaching Mike at the same time demanded her total attention, allowing her a measure of inner peace. Until she returned to the ranch . . .

Ben managed to spend every moment possible near her. By hiring two more ranch hands, he had lightened his own work load. With time on his hands, he lingered over Emma's meals, and after dinner he sprawled comfortably in the living room as Sami read to her nieces.

By the last week of June, Ben had had a larger bathroom built next to her bedroom. The room was light and airy, with lush carpeting. When Ben opened the door to show it to her, he nodded toward the enormous pink bathtub. The intensity of his stare brought a blushing warmth to her cheeks. "This is your bathroom, Sami. It's a bit oversized for you alone, maybe," he said. "But I've always liked a lot of room."

He moved closer to her, and Sami's heart started beating faster. Suddenly, the large room seemed too small. His intimate suggestion that they share the tub had sent her imagination into overdrive. Ben had all the markings of a sensuous man, and he knew how to reach into her as he had done on the night of their ride.

"The room is beautiful, Ben," she said in an effort to keep their intimacy on an even keel and to ease her inner tension. He was on the prowl again, and each time he neared her, her heart began to race and her legs felt unsteady.

His fingertips caressed the nape of her neck as they stood in the spacious, mirror-lined bathroom. While their mirrored reflections stared back at them, he stroked the underside of her chin.

"I hoped you'd like it. But it needs a woman's touch. Would you mind decorating it?"

"I'd love to, Ben," Sami managed as her heart

seemed to turn over. Ben's smile was definitely a potential danger to her internal systems. Right now, she felt like a teenager about to launch her first romance.

She teasingly reminded him of his blunt statement when she had first arrived. "But I thought you didn't want things changed. Didn't you once say something about me being a woman who liked things to suit her?" Now, why had she said that? They had been talking of decorating—of soap dishes and wallpaper.

Ben's eyes darkened. "Well, *I've* changed my mind, honey."

The desire sharpening his features caused Sami's knees to weaken. Unable to force her eyes from his, she whispered, "Ben, I . . ."

"You're a beautiful woman, Sami," he said huskily. "Intelligent. Warm. I get the feeling sometimes, that you're not real. That you're too good to be true. But I'm damned glad you're here. Now," he added in a whisper that caused Sami to grip the edge of the vanity for support, "how much longer are you going to make me wait to see if the dream is real, pretty lady?"

- 6 -

THE FIRST WEEK of July, Sami sat on a knoll overlooking the ranch yard. After Mike's last afternoon class, he had announced that he and Judy had a date. Sami had chosen not to paint, but to relax in the sun. Its heat remained in the red rock she leaned against. The cool dampness of the earth began to penetrate the thick padding of pine needles and the blanket beneath her.

She watched Ben run the long distance from the barn doorway to the backyard, Chug frolicking about his long legs. Astride Ben's wide shoulders, Lori laughed and locked her arms around his head while Mary Jane bounced in the crook of his arm.

Ben's sprint was that of a much younger man, and Sami remembered Mike's favorite term for his father. "The old man," she said aloud, and thought that nothing about Ben was old—not his physical appearance, his thoughts, his desires.

In the last week, he had stalked Sami with his eyes, with the casual brush of his hand across the back of hers, with the nudge of his knee beneath the supper table. And when Mike and Judy set off the Fourth of July fireworks, Ben's hand had slipped to her shoulder and she'd felt him watching her. He was too close and too dangerous to her emotional safety.

As the purple mountain shadows swept across the ranch yard, Sami followed Lori and Mary Jane's antics on the tree swing Ben had rigged up in the yard. They both crawled into the old tire suspended from heavy ropes, faced each other, and began to rock the swing as they chanted. The bough overhead began to quake; the tire swung higher.

Emma's down-home cooking had rounded out their bodies, Sami realized. They were rosy-cheeked and happy, often dragging Mike or Ben into a two-against-one battle in the living room or making Ben read them bedtime stories before they would kiss him good night. He took as much interest in the children's activities as he did in his son's studies.

"Ben Woden," Sami said involuntarily, as she thought about the man. She tightened her grip about her knees and leaned back against the warm red rock behind her. She tugged Mike's flannel-lined denim jacket closer about her shoulders, lifting the heavy fall of hair trapped beneath it to spread over the worn cloth.

Mike herded the children into the house, and Ben vanished into the barn. An hour passed as Sami contentedly watched the layers of scarlet and blue-gray sky settle above the rugged peaks while the sun sank toward the mountains.

"Jim Bridger and the first trappers must have felt the same way, Sami." She hadn't heard the pine needles rustle or felt the tall length of Ben's body settle beside her. He leaned against the rock supporting her back and stretched his long legs before him. "Beautiful country. Wild country. Time seems to stop here."

"It is beautiful," she agreed.

"I hated it once," he said thoughtfully. "Ran away from it and from Pa."

Sami glanced at his masculine profile. She wanted to know more about him. "Tell me about it."

He shifted more comfortably on her folded blanket, and his shoulder brushed hers. "It was a long time ago." He laced his fingers with hers and rested them in his lap. "It doesn't matter anymore. Your hands are cold, little bit."

"Tell me, Ben," she persisted.

"Only if I can hold you. You can ask me anything then."

A knife-sharp pang slashed at Sami's insides. "Now, Ben . . ." But before she finished the protest, one strong arm swept beneath her to lift her to his lap.

She squirmed as his left hand quickly circled her wrists.

"Hey, I should have tried this before." The pleasure in his voice stroked her sensually. "You've sidestepped me all week, little bit. And I think I know why someone as cool and as self-assured as you would tremble when a man comes near you."

"Ben, let me go!" She'd fought the attraction of her body to his for weeks, and her resistance was wearing thin. "Ben!" His mouth slid down the sensitive cords of her neck, raising a heated trail. "Ben, you were going to tell me about—Oh!" The tip of his tongue trailed up to her earlobe. "Ah, Ben, you were going to tell me about . . ." He traced the convolutions of her ear, his breath warm and moist within it.

"Mmm." The gravelly rasp vibrated against her cheek as he nuzzled it. "Ask away."

With Sami's soft warmth nestled against him, the pain of his childhood was not as poignant. He had lived with the bitter memory of too much work, long hours, and makeshift meals for many years. Now, as he told Sami of his life, he felt relieved.

He saw his own feeling reflected in her wide brown

eyes; he drowned in the compassion written across her beautiful face. His lips continued to speak, but his jaw tingled as her palm glided up to cradle it. He leaned against the softness. "My first wife and I were kids when we got married. Mae didn't know much about making a home for Mike, and I sure as hell didn't have the training. Janelle, my second wife, was a good enough stepmother, but we were never really in love."

The tip of her finger investigated his bottom lip, tugged it gently. He felt his desire rise, hardening his body. His skin quivered where the gentle probe of her fingers touched. "Ah . . . Sami." Lord, she was so small and delicate. To make love with her . . .

"Ah . . . what?" Sami murmured, loving the rough texture of his skin as she slid her fingers over the shape of his jaw. Ben quivered at her first experimental touch, and his reaction excited her, heated the blood rushing up to her cheeks. But now the smoke-gray eyes were wary, his great body restless and taut beneath hers. He moved away from the feather-light touches across the rawboned planes of his face.

"You're . . . ah," he groaned as she wove the sable thickness of his hair through her fingers.

Sami had never played the temptress, but now the game was exciting and she found she rather liked being the aggressor.

"Kiss me, Ben." The desperation within her formed the words as she tilted her face upward. She needed Ben. The thought of his large body pressing into hers excited her, and she acknowledged her strong physical response to him. For just this one evening, she would be the woman he wanted. She needed—had to have—Ben. She tugged his head down to hers and murmured, "Love me, Ben."

In answer, Ben's lips settled lightly, reverently, on hers. The strong arms enfolding her trembled, his heartbeat slammed unevenly against her breast. His tone was teasing, flirtatious. "At my age, don't you think making love to you might prove too much for me?"

"Don't be shy, Ben." She liked the intimate playfulness, the boyish side of this rough cowboy. She tugged the lobe of his ear and nestled deeper into the heat of his lap. "I'll be gentle."

"Shoot! I'm the one who has to worry about being gentle." The real concern in his voice brought Sami's eyes to his. Ben was just . . . just suddenly there to enjoy. His desire was evident beneath her hips, and when he shifted uncomfortably, Sami twisted around to straddle his upper thighs. She tilted her head to the side, fascinated by the red flush creeping up his sinewy neck. The big fingers pressed deep into her waist as she eased her breasts against his muscled chest. She locked her arms firmly about his shoulders and rubbed the tip of his nose with hers.

Ben's sharply indrawn breath was her reward. His left hand spanned her back beneath the jacket, and he stroked the length of her spine slowly, down, then up. Lightly, the weight of his hand swept downward to rest on her buttocks. Through the denim, she felt his palm tremble, then firmly shape her softness.

"You're playing with fire, lady," he said roughly against her lips. "You'll have your regrets in the morning."

When her tongue traveled the unrelenting contour of his upper lip, Ben groaned, and Sami felt a shudder pass through the large, tense body beneath her. She licked her bottom lip, savored the sweet taste clinging to her tongue. "You taste like bubble gum."

He pressed kisses into one corner of her mouth, then the other. "Um-hmm. The girls and I had a contest to see who could blow the biggest bubble."

She feathered kisses across the coarseness of his brows, the thick fringe of his eyelashes, and down the enticingly crooked bridge of his nose. "How did you break your nose? A rodeo fall?"

His hands fit nicely into her waistband, sliding around to the front, the hair on the back of his hands slightly tickling her stomach. "Uh-uh. More like the back of a chair during a tavern brawl."

"Ben! You didn't get hit in the face with a chair? That's awful! You won, didn't you?" she asked as his hands spread across her back.

He growled, easing her down on her back and following her with the full-length sprawl of his body. He deftly arranged the blanket beneath them, half-lifting Sami as he did so. "Of course I won. Good guys always win. It's the law of the West."

Somehow his legs tangled with hers as he settled lightly over her, his head and shoulders blocking out the setting sun. Sami ran her hands over the tenseness of his shoulders, felt the big body ripple against hers as she did so. Ben watched her, desire stamped on his expression. "Little bit," he murmured roughly.

"Cowboy," she answered, loving the heavy feel of his chest flattening her breasts, excited by the hardness arching against her hips. If only just for tonight, she had to be his woman.

His kiss was all that she hoped for: a tender hunger that homed in on her mouth, exploding the heat coiling at the base of her stomach. She locked her arms about him, held him near until she just had to explore his masculine geography. Her fingers traveled down the muscled sweep of his back to the slight rise of his hips, fluttered with the temptation to caress his muscular buttocks. Her hands rose to research the wide, wide shoulders.

Braced by his elbows, Ben searched for the fullness of her breasts, gently cupped his palms over them, and took an unsteady, deep breath. "You're exquisite, Sami. I want to see you."

Her trembling hands found the buttons of his shirt, quickly eased them open until his shirt fluttered free. Despite the certainty of his hands, the callused fingertips grazed her skin as he began to unbutton her blouse. His gaze left hers as he stared down at her breasts. Slowly, he lowered his head to kiss the sweet hollow at the base of her neck, then trailed his lips across her collarbones to rest momentarily in the valley of her softness.

He kissed her white cotton bra, traveling a course toward the crest of a breast. The moist enclosure of his mouth settled over her nipple, dampening the cloth covering it, as his teeth delicately worried the hardened nub.

"Ben!" Fire encased Sami, placed the cool evening air beyond the heat of their bodies. Shafts of white-hot lava seemed to flow through her legs, even as they thrust against his restlessly. His heavy, ragged breath encircled her ear as he quickly removed her blouse and jeans, the sweep of his palms sensitizing her flesh where he touched.

"Now undress me, Sami," he urged as he nuzzled aside her bra strap and spread wildfire kisses over the swell of her breast. Behind her, his fingers searched for the clasp, and suddenly the unbound fullness of her breasts pressed against the heated planes of his chest. Sami gasped, feeling her softness shape itself to his body. Her hunger grew; she yearned for the hardness of his legs against her.

"Ah, Ben . . ." Her palms smoothed his taut stomach. *Just for this moment . . .*

And then his hot, hard body thrust against her softness as she removed his clothing. Clad only in her white cotton briefs, Sami could not breathe as his palm swept slowly down her legs. His fingertips grazed her sensitive inner thighs in their upward journey, then pressed against her abdomen. "You're so soft, Sami. And as sweet-smelling as field clover."

She lifted the wave of hair drifting down across his brow, urged it back into the sable thickness with her fingers. "You're quite a hunk, Benjamin," she said softly as she searched for his lips. She needed his kiss to send away all the nightmares—her father's mistreatment of her and the painful loss of her husband.

His tongue entered her mouth, foraged for the sweetness there, as he settled his body completely over hers. His desire thrust against her stomach, imprinting her with his need. "And you are quite a lady, Sami. I want you so much."

He eased her briefs from her, touched the hollow of her hipbones delicately, reverently. Then he laughed shakily. "I imagined we'd make love for the first time in a king-sized bed. I fantasized you hungry for me, like that first night at your trailer."

Sami stroked his powerful calf with her instep, easing her hips lower. When the probing heat of Ben's manhood rested between her thighs, she sighed contentedly.

"Hell. I can't stand much more of this, little bit. I haven't had a woman for a long time. Haven't wanted one." He groaned. "I'm afraid I'll hurt you."

Locked in her own passion, Sami held him closer, raising her hips slightly to meet the heated tip of his desire. "I want you, cowboy," she whispered.

Gently, Ben eased fully into her moistness, then halted. His eyes closed, his expression one of intense pleasure as he lifted his head. "You're so small, honey. I'll be careful . . ."

Sami luxuriated in his fullness and shifted to accept him more deeply. "It's been a long time for me, too, darling." As they lay quietly, wrapped in each other's arms, Sami stroked the back of his taut neck, played with the damp tendrils. Ben was holding back, his body beginning to tremble with the effort of controlling his passion. He nuzzled the side of her neck, not allowing his weight to settle more heavily on her.

"So soft . . ." he said shakily. "Like warm velvet. I feel like I'm in heaven."

"You're not in heaven yet, Ben," Sami teased as she smiled against the dampness of his temple.

He raised himself up on an elbow, smoothed her hair back from her face. Tenderly, he smiled down at her, tracing his forefinger downward to touch her erect nipple. The hot coil inside her tightened as he shifted higher into her. His smile was all male pleasure. "I've been a long time without a woman, honey. I'm just getting into the mood."

He withdrew a fraction, and Sami gasped, "Ben!"

He gazed down at her solemnly. "Our first time, honey." He slid back into her fully, his left hand caressing the softness of her breasts. "You're beautiful. Perfect, right down to the sweetness of these."

She gasped as his tongue laved the darkened aureola of each breast. When his lips curved around one to suckle it, invisible cords tugged Sami's body toward his. She thrust herself up as his hips pressed the softness of hers, his mouth seeking, drawing her nipple within the hot moistness. "Ben . . ." Her sigh was captured by his mouth fitting over hers.

Ben raised her to the ultimate goal, stroking her body as she soared into a world where only he existed, then eased her gently back to reality in his trembling arms. Later, wrapped in Ben's arms, she nuzzled the damp planes of his chest. "Mmm, fuzzy."

Somewhere over her head, Ben managed a deep, ragged sigh. "Don't get playful. I'm still recovering." With an effort, he flipped one corner of the blanket over their tangled legs and tucked Sami's discarded coat about her back and shoulders. "I don't want you to catch a chill, honey."

Beneath her cheek, the heavy beat of his heart had slowed to normal; the weight of his arm crossing her back was pleasantly heavy. Sami felt as though she could float over the pine trees to the moon. She explored the flatness of his nipples with her index finger.

Ben stroked her hip in a leisurely fashion. "That was

some gift, lady. You're white-hot when you love. Despite your tiny size, you're exhausting, honey." His hand pressed against her ribs. "I can see your little smirk down there. Pleased with yourself, aren't you?" He kissed the fragrant dampness of her temple, nuzzled the fine hair there.

Sami smoothed his flat stomach with her palm, enjoying the lazy afterglow of their passion. "You see, you didn't need to worry about hurting me."

Ben snorted, his massive chest lifting beneath her cheek. "No, but I had things planned a lot different, little bit. You just took me a little too fast for me to back up."

She half lifted herself above him. "Benjamin Wade Woden, are you saying I seduced you?"

His grin was rueful. "Well, yeah. I guess so." His expression stilled as she frowned. "Oh, now, little bit. Don't go getting all het up." He stroked the smooth sweep of her back. "You've done nothing improper. I just wasn't prepared for a white-hot, raven-haired witch loving the holy daylights out of me."

"Ben—"

"Sami." His voice dropped to a serious tone. "I can't bear to think any man has hurt you, honey."

It was time to tell him about her father.

Settling down against him, Sami stared at the stars overhead, breathed the pine fragrance permeating the cool night air. With his strong, warm body sheltering hers, his hand stroking the long sweep of her hair, she felt secure. Her childhood in Arkansas seemed to have happened to someone else. "The big man who hurt me was my own father, Ben. He was the bull of the woods in the backwoods community we lived in. When he was done beating our mother, he'd come looking for my sister Ann and me. He always found us . . ."

She shuddered, and Ben's arms tightened about her. "At thirteen, I ran away, leaving my baby sister to fend for herself; our mother was dead by then. I had two choices—to hit the road or to marry Jimmy, a man just like my father. I was sent to a series of foster homes, and I learned later that Ann had married Jimmy. There but for the grace of God . . ." She shuddered.

His warm fingers caressed her shoulder. "Tell me about your own husband."

Sami was still shaken by her volcanic response to Ben—and he seemed to be pushing her once more. She shifted uncomfortably against him. She did not want to discuss Des—she still hadn't adjusted to the newness of her intimacy with Ben. "I loved him," she said simply.

"He must have been a special person, then." Ben spoke carefully.

"I was comfortable with him. We had mutual interests: art, plays, gourmet cooking, books. And he was charming, witty—I was drawn to him."

Beside her, Ben tensed and stirred restlessly. His tone was bitter as he said, "I see. A cultural meeting of the minds."

She eased herself up, tugged the jacket around her, covering her breasts. She hadn't liked his summation of her marriage. And he had definitely chosen the wrong time to forage into her conjugal past. She had barely adjusted to the idea of being his lover.

Damn, Ben thought. He resented not being able to share the things that were important to her. He'd worked hard all his life, and now he felt as though he fell short of Sami's expectations. It was a damned uncomfortable feeling. But something had set her on edge.

He wanted her back in his arms again, and tried to soothe her. "Oh, now, little bit." His hand found the roundness of her knee, his thumb caressing the inner flesh. "You're getting that mulish look. When your bottom lip pouts like that, I know you're getting set to dig in your heels. Cool down."

"'Cool down'? You make me sound like . . . like some contrary horse!"

Ben adjusted the loose flap of the blanket about his

hips and rolled to his side. He knew from her expression that he'd said the wrong thing again. Despite her size, Sami could be as formidable as his new bull when she set her mind to it. They'd just shared as intimate a moment as a man and a woman could share, her sensual needs surprising him. Her instincts had been natural and beautiful as she gave herself to him, pleasing him beyond what he had thought possible. He rubbed his palm across his jaw, thinking. Flushed, still warm from their lovemaking, Sami seemed affronted. *What had he said to upset her?*

She edged away from him and began to look for her clothing amid the scattered piles. Moonlight caught her face as she turned, and Ben read her disgust, her anger. It ignited his own. "Sami, so help me. If you think we shared a roll in the hay a moment ago and that's all, you're wrong. It was something pretty special."

Trying to conceal her breasts as she tugged on her jeans, Sami sent him a scathing glance. "I suppose you've had enough sex to tell the difference. *I*, of course, have only been with one man before, and don't possess your worldly knowledge."

"Damn right." Disoriented by her changed mood, Ben trusted his primitive instincts. She was *his* woman. He reached for her, but she turned her back and slipped into Mike's jacket. He held her upper arm as she tried to stand, bracing his weight on his other elbow. "We didn't just have sex, lady. We made love."

Her eyes widened, the shock of his statement traveling the length of her body. Love. Ben was pushing her again. She needed time to unravel her new relationship with him. But Ben not only wanted to explore her marriage, he wanted a commitment from her. Now—tonight. She straightened slowly when he released her, staring down at him. "It was propinquity."

"Lady, I don't know what that word means, but it doesn't sound good." Ben's jaw hardened, his eyes narrowing dangerously.

"It means we've lived so close together this past month that a certain amount of sexual tension has developed between us." Ben needed to be put in his place, she thought. And he needed to think twice about charging into the intimate corners of her life. She shrugged. "What just happened simply served the needs of two adults, male and female. I must be getting back. What time is it?"

"Who the hell cares what time it is?" Ben roared, feeling as if he'd been stomped by a bull. He rummaged for his jeans, grabbed them, and stood. The sharp pine needles stung his feet as he jammed his left leg, then his right one, into his jeans. He fastened the snap, placed his fists on his hips, and glared down at her.

"You're being unreasonable, Ben." The cool, clipped tone was the same one she used on Mike and the girls when they misbehaved. "We shared a moment of mutual pleasure. Mike is doing well, and the children and I will be on our way in a couple of months."

Ben felt his mouth go dry at the thought of her absence. "Like hell you will." If it weren't for what she had just given him, maybe he'd have let Sami return to her well-ordered life. But not now, he vowed. No way.

"Let's get home. Emma said she'd keep supper waiting for you," he growled as he hunted for his boots. If Sami Lassiter thought she could just bow quietly out of his life in a few months, she had another think coming. He didn't aim to let her go . . . not ever.

- 7 -

"I WAS RIGHT, Ben. Auntie sleeps on her tummy, and she wears a T-shirt." Lori's adamant voice carried down to Sami as she nuzzled her pillow. "I won the bet. And I want my quarter now."

Sami forced open one eyelid, caught sight of worn denim covering a masculine knee, and scooted down into the depths of her patchwork quilt. "Auntie!" Lori squealed. "Where are you going?"

Sami murmured a very unladylike word and pulled her pillow into the opening of her blanket cave as if it were the stopper on a thermos. Her sleep-warm skin tingled, her stomach knotting as she heard Ben's low chuckle. "She's like a turtle, isn't she?" His palm patted the blanket over Sami's backside. "See? She's even shaped like one."

"Ha, ha! Auntie's a turtle, Auntie's a turtle. We're gonna go tell Emma and Mikey that Auntie's a turtle," Mary Jane chanted singsong fashion as she and Lori skipped from the room.

The large hand caressed her bottom once more, then slid up her spine. "Come out of there, sunshine. It's morning; I thought we'd ride out to watch the sunrise."

"Ben, get out of here before I throw something at you." The Hun invasion couldn't have compared to this, Sami thought wildly, trying to assemble her jumbled thoughts. It was bad enough he had chased her in her dreams, but the reality of Ben actually sitting down on her bed . . .

Her mattress dipped with his weight, rolling Sami toward him. He caught her waist, holding her immobile with one hand as he tugged the corner of the quilt back from her face with his other hand. "Ben, I'm warning you. I'm not in the mood for this."

His forefinger swirled a long strand of hair that had fallen across her cheek, easing it behind her ear. Sami half turned to glare at him. Had she not been so angry, she would have acknowledged the tenderness in his expression. But she was mad; she wasn't ready to face him this morning.

Sami was still shaken by her passionate reaction to his lovemaking. She wanted to deal privately with her emotions. Perhaps her biological clock had just struck the right hour in her life, she thought. It had been so long since she had made love. After all, Ben was a tender, volcanic lover. Conceivably, she might care for him. But she needed time to explore her fiery reaction to him, to place it in balance with the rest of her life.

But Ben had all the markings of a pleased, confident lover this morning, when she had not yet adjusted to their new relationship. One more time, he had her off balance. Surely *no one* ever dealt with complex feelings at dawn, she grumbled to herself.

Then she frowned at Ben. She felt like a rumpled sock at the bottom of a laundry basket, waiting to be folded. Ben, on the other hand, was freshly shaven and wearing a wide grin. She had never understood "morning people," and she would *never* understand Ben . . . even after she'd had her second cup of coffee.

"How are you feeling this morning, little bit?" he asked. Angry as she was, the sensual rumble of his voice tugged at her heart, tightened her lower belly, and heated her limbs.

"Fine. I like having people invade the privacy of my bedroom before the sun is up. I'm just fine," she gritted between tightly clamped teeth. But she wasn't fine. She ached in some very feminine places as well as in the muscles of her arms and legs. She remembered clinging to him with every ounce of her strength as they scaled the peak of their lovemaking. "Go away, Ben."

His hand stroked down the length of her leg, smoothing the quilt covering her. "I didn't realize you were grumpy in the morning, honey," he murmured lazily. His hand traveled up the length of her other leg, smoothed the shape of her hips lightly. "But then, there are a lot of things I don't know about you."

"You're none too sweet, either," she shot back. *Why did he have to happen in her life?* She loved her independence, enjoyed not being accountable to anyone but herself. She'd had her life neatly compartmentalized until he'd come along, tearing down the walls she'd built around her heart. She turned toward him more fully, keeping the quilt pulled beneath her chin, and eyed him calculatingly. His mouth seemed fuller, more sensuous than it had been a moment before, and the smoky gray eyes darkened as he stared down into her own eyes.

The spicy smell of after shave lingered about her nose, which was half tucked into the down pillow. Water droplets from a recent shower glistened on his dark chest hair; his clothes smelled as though they had just come from Emma's clothesline.

Every lean ounce of him spoke of masculine confidence, as though he'd won his victory and had come to collect the spoils. Sami did not feel like being the object of his warm, sexy smile this morning. She resented his air of possession.

The rough fingertip trailing down her warm cheek caused her to shiver. Her teeth nibbled at her bottom lip as she tried to decide how to dislodge Ben Woden from her room. He was twice her size, with more moves in his repertoire than a stallion who'd been loose on the range too long.

"What are you thinking, brown-eyes?" A corner of his mouth slanted upward, and the lines radiating from his eyes deepened.

Much as she wanted to, she couldn't say, *Mister, you scratch my back the wrong way. You rile me until I don't care if the sun doesn't shine*. What she did say was, "If you will please leave my room, I'll get dressed."

"Sami, what's going on in there?" he asked seriously, his hand stroking her hair. "From your expression, it looks like your wheels and cogs are all turning in different directions."

"You're in my room at dawn, taking up half my bed, and you wonder what's wrong?" she asked indignantly.

He smiled ruefully. "I thought you'd be in a grouchy mood when you woke up. I see I didn't miss my bet."

Who was he anyway, to bet on how she woke up? Sami felt anger begin to simmer within her. A lady never displayed the passionate antagonism she now felt for this rancher, she reminded herself.

But her thoughts passed her lips before she could stop them. "I just flat out don't like you, Ben."

The heavy brows lifted to the wave crossing his forehead, but the tender amusement in his expression did not alter. "Really?"

She felt like old Engine Number Nine, stoked up and ready to roll down the tracks, smokestacks blowing full steam. "You've got to realize that things just . . . happen sometimes. Then they're done."

She didn't like the twinkle in those gray eyes, not one bit. "It's past. A fluke—"

"Never to happen again in a coon's age?"

"Right." She hadn't meant to get into this discussion now, but since she had, she saw no reason not to finish it once and for all. "It's not that you're too old, Ben. Or that you're half the size of a house with too much experience gained from heaven knows where—"

"I know. I looked up your word in the dictionary. What happened was the result of propinquity, right?" He tossed her own explanation back at her.

"Well, yes. I suppose so."

She wished he hadn't smiled then. At least not that kind of smile, suggesting that he knew all the rules of the game and that she was just a beginner.

Engine Number Nine slowed down. Ben's silvery gaze flicked across her face. "Hmmm," he drawled.

Before Sami could determine what his "hmmm" meant, he looked around the pansy-printed hominess of her room. Emma had donated a supply of chicken-feed sacks—preprinted cotton with pretty flowers—and the treadle sewing maching so Sami could sew the girls' clothes. She had made the curtains from the leftover material.

"Very feminine. Exactly how I thought you would decorate it."

As he turned to examine the plant starts on the windowsill, the quilt beneath him shifted. Sami grabbed it with both hands, tugging it back up to her neck. "Get out!"

Ben studied the wild play of her black hair across the violet-printed pillow for a long moment. The intensity of his stare seemed to draw the air from Sami's lungs momentarily. His gaze moved to the canvases leaning against the wall. Mike's large and vibrantly colored landscapes overpowered the smaller, more delicately hued paintings she had done herself.

"Are those Mike's?" Ben studied the bold portrayals intently. "Yours are very good, but Mike's are—"

While Sami knew her own work was salable, she

also knew Mike's paintings demonstrated true genius. She elaborated on Ben's thought. "Mike's a gifted artist, Ben. He has a natural insight to the wild beauty of the mountains. He paints with his heart and soul, and his work reflects his love for the land. He only needed some basic instruction in the use of acrylics. If he continues, his work will be in great demand. Someday it might even be hung in museums."

"He's that good? My God." The sigh contained a father's pride. "Thank you, Sami," he said simply. His tender gaze caused Sami's heartbeat to accelerate.

"Mike's talent is his own. He would have found it sooner or later." Shivers raced up her backbone as Ben continued to study every contour of her face. She didn't like his ability to lift the corners of her emotions, peek beneath her control. His vulnerability about his son was genuine; she respected it. But it raised a responsive tenderness within her that she couldn't afford to feel.

"Please leave, Ben. I have a lot of work to do today. Mike and I have to frame our paintings before we take them to the Lone Pine Art Gallery this afternoon. Several of our works are going to hang in the local artists' show."

A dark flush rose in Ben's hollow cheeks as his brows formed a single threatening line. "And I suppose I'm not invited."

So much for vulnerability; so much for tenderness, she thought. "Of course you are. Eileen called yesterday morning. The president of the local art club asked her if she knew any local artists not already participating in the show. They have more display space than expected. It was a last-minute thing, and Mike hasn't had a chance to ask you yet. You're his father and—"

"Your lover." The pugnacious jut of his freshly shaven jaw dared her to deny the claim. Sami felt as if her blood slowed, then came to a full stop in her veins.

"Do you have to be so blunt?"

"It's a fact, lady. We made love last night. That makes me your lover."

"Ben Woden!" Sami gasped indignantly.

"Sami Lassiter," he returned in a drawl. "You'd better get your cute little backside out of this sack . . . before I start thinking you want me in it with you."

"When sows fly! That will be the day, Mr. Woden!"

"I love it when your Arkie talk slips out, little bit." He chuckled. "Come on, let's get started. You can teach me how to frame a painting."

After an eleven o'clock lunch, Sami glared at the back of Ben's arrogant head as she sat in the Bronco's rear seat. And when Mike attempted light conversation, she glared at him, too, just for good measure. Ben's wink at his son irritated her, as did his explanation. "She woke up that way. Doesn't seem to be a cheery person in the early morning."

They arrived at the community center just in time to hang the paintings in the designated spaces. Sami was so busy directing the Woden males to hang them properly that she forgot her urge to drape one of the canvases over Ben's head. The judges arrived at one o'clock to pronounce Mike the most promising artist of the show. Sami's paintings earned the accolade of "most accomplished technique."

Ben seemed at ease, laughing and talking with various townspeople. Whenever Sami glanced at him, his smoky gaze locked with hers. *Lover,* he had said, and now the heated stroke of his eyes held a lover's promise. Sami's skin heated as she forced her stare from his.

At three o'clock, Mike grabbed her hand and tugged her into a corner. He nodded at a well-dressed man, who smiled back at them. "That guy wants to buy four of my pictures, Sami. Can you believe it? What do I do now?"

"You name a price, Mike. Set it high. You can always come down."

Mike's excited expression stilled, then died. Sami followed the path of his eyes to four rough-looking young men. The leather-skirted, tousle-haired girl with them bore a hardened look. "Those are the guys, and the girl is Becky Westfield."

His fists tightened at his sides, his dark coloring paling. "They're here to make trouble, aren't they, Mike?" Sami asked quietly.

"Yeah. They've been riding me hard. They think painting is sissy stuff."

Sami saw Ben's wide shoulders approaching, easing through the small groups of people who stood between them. His expression was that of an avenging giant. "Mike, stop your dad. I'll handle this," Sami whispered as she stepped toward the toughs.

"Can I help you?" she asked the apparent leader.

"Yeah, I'd like that." His leer traced her prim white blouse with its billowy sleeves and large navy bow tie.

"Dad, stop," Mike whispered roughly a few feet away as the youth's eyes sauntered down the length of Sami's navy skirt to her medium-high heels.

When the leader's gaze lifted to her tightly pinned, twisted hair, Sami smiled her most charming smile. "I'll bet you came to see Mike's work. He's going to be famous one day, and you'll be able to say you knew him. Would you come this way?"

"Oh, yeah. We'd just *love* to, lady," the girl said in a bored tone.

"My name is Sami." She extended her hand. "What's yours?" Reluctantly, the teenagers shook her hand and introduced themselves.

"Mike is really good," Sami confided as she led them to Mike's pictures. "You're all going to be proud of him."

The leader studied the paintings, sucking his teeth as

he mulled the familiar scenery. "Looks okay to me," he judged finally.

"You have good taste," Sami said, and added a smile. "Are you an artist, too? I'll bet you are. You have that sensitive look about the eyes." She studied the youth's face for a moment. "You look like Michael Douglas, the movie star."

He snorted, then chuckled. "Lady, you're full of it."

Sami laughed, enjoying the way the young man's expression had changed from a scowl to a grin. "Says you."

One of the other youths stepped closer. "What's the deal with Mike's dad? Are you his old lady?"

Sami glanced at Ben's lowered brows, the tightened line of his mouth. "I wouldn't touch him today with a ten-foot pole."

"He's got no couth, huh?" The youth grinned down at her. "You're little but you're tough."

Sami couldn't help laughing, and the rest joined her. "Okay, the food is over there, guys," she said. "Help yourself."

When the show was finally over, Ben slammed the back door of the Bronco closed. "All your paintings are packed inside, Sami. I bought every last one, and I don't feel like arguing about it."

His brusque mood had begun when Sami chatted with the youths. His scowl had deepened throughout the afternoon until the five o'clock closing time. "Mike's riding home with Judy Thacker." He stalked to the passenger side of the vehicle, jerked open the door. "Get in. I don't have all day. I'm hungry. We're going to Fred's Diner."

"Prince Charming," Sami muttered as Ben crossed to the driver's side and slid into the seat.

Fred's Diner had more trucks than cars in its parking lot. The marquee advertised MUD WRESTLING AND WET

T-SHIRT CONTEST TONIGHT. Jukebox music blared over the loud rumble of voices as Ben ushered her into the crowded tavern. Sami noticed that Ben's leather jacket and pressed slacks contrasted with the cotton shirts and blue jeans worn by the other men. The flat of his hand rested on the small of her back as he guided her to a table in the center of the smoke-filled room.

"Hey, Ben. Long time no see," a voice yelled from somewhere in the distance as Ben seated her. He waved in the direction of the call, then yelled in another direction, "Two steaks over here."

Sami couldn't see anything past the several sets of brawny shoulders surrounding their table. She was determined to relax and wait out the evening. She folded her hands in her lap and thought that she needed as little confrontration as possible tonight—with Ben, or with anyone.

"They serve good steaks here." Ben's expression dared her to argue the fact. "You're mad, aren't you?"

She stared at him. Of course she was mad. "A little around the edges. You bought all my pictures, and now people will gossip for certain. And you did nothing but glower at me. On top of that, when Eddie and I were talking, you acted like the U.S. Cavalry charging to the rescue."

The youth had actually paled as Ben had descended on them. Crossing his arms, Ben had glared at Eddie until the young man withdrew to his friends.

"That punk put his arm around you."

"He touched my shoulder, Mr. Woden."

"In my day, we called it a pass, lady."

"So?" Sami really didn't want to glare back at him. She just wanted the harrowing day to end. She was tired and she needed to relax in a hot bath with a good book. Ben Woden did not salve her frayed nerves.

A round of shouts shot up to her left, and a woman screamed. Men rose from the tables, surging as one body toward the commotion. A waitress jostled her way between the men and placed water glasses and salad bowls carefully on Ben and Sami's table.

"Rosie is mud wrestling tonight," the waitress stated. "She asked Johnnie to put Jell-O or pudding in the wrestling pit, but he nixed that idea. She just won the match with Lisa and—oh-oh . . ."

The waitress inched behind Ben. "Rosie is upset because you haven't been around, Ben. After you took her out a couple times, she thought you two were a steady item," she whispered quickly. "She's been telling everyone that you're her guy. She just saw you, and she's headed this way."

"Damn," Ben muttered. "I tied one on after a rodeo last fall and woke up at her place the next morning. We were a hot item for all of two weeks. But if we're having a romance, it's news to me."

Stalking toward their table, shoving aside the good-natured male fans, was an Amazon—Rosie, fresh from the wrestling pit. Mud clung to her wet T-shirt and shorts, which revealed more voluptuous curves than they concealed. Arms akimbo, the giantess stopped before Ben. "So. Where have you been, Ben?" she asked.

The wrestler glanced down at Sami. Rosie looked as though she wanted to tear something apart. "Is this your new woman, Ben? You used to like 'em with more meat on their bones," she stated baldly. "Is she why you haven't been around to see me?"

Rosie's tone was challenging, her eyes narrowing down at Sami. The woman's lack of subtlety grated on Sami's nerves. This encounter with Ben's jealous ex-lover was the perfect climax to her day, Sami thought ruefully. She wanted to be in her bath, counting bubbles and the tiny rosebuds on the wallpaper. She looked about for a hole to drop into and found none.

Ben had the grace to blush as he flicked a silent apology at her. One more day in the further adventures of Sami Lassiter, Sami thought as she heard Ben introduce Rosie to her. "She's teaching Mike," he concluded.

Rosie eased closer. She glanced down at the clots of mud plopping steadily over Sami's dress shoes, and smiled cynically. "Teacher. Is that what they call it now?" she asked, inching closer. A large brown glob spattered down the length of Sami's full, white sleeve. The wrestler shook her long, mud-coated hair. A fine spray shot across Sami's prim blouse, and Rosie's nasty grin widened.

Sami leaped to her feet just as Ben rose. His hand wrapped about Rosie's upper arm to detain her as she took a step toward Sami.

"Woden! Git your hands off my woman," roared a huge man, who was charging through the crowd toward them.

"Fight! Fight! I'll take odds on Woden right here! Place your bets." The man's call sounded just as Sami caught sight of a fist swinging over her head. When it collided with Ben's jaw, she didn't have time to ponder the crunch of knuckle and bone, or to politely say, "No, thank you," to Rosie before the tossed salad landed on top of her neatly coiled hair. She flicked a lettuce leaf from her eyes just in time to see Rosie's hands thrusting at her shoulders. And then she fell into the mud pit.

The mud was slimy on her bottom and the backs of her legs, saturating her clothing. It oozed between her fingers, cool and smooth, unlike the emotions boiling within her. She'd had enough. There was only one thing she could do now—fight.

"Okay, you asked for it," she heard herself say as she kicked off her heels and tugged free her bedraggled bow tie.

"Ah, forget it," Rosie grumbled. "Ben couldn't possibly be interested in an underdeveloped body like yours. It just galled me to see you sitting with him when I been waiting for him to come around. I can't wrestle you. It wouldn't be a fair match: You're half my size! Now that I've seen you, I know Ben will be back when he wants a real woman."

Sami didn't care what was fair. She was past debating the matter. Rosie's insults had gone too far, and she had to pay.

Sami felt her body tighten, her heart pumping steadily, much as it had when she was on the mat in the martial arts course she'd once taken. She'd been fast and agile and determined, winning matches over much larger opponents.

"Uh! Ah . . ." Sami heard pained grunts and furniture splintering in the distance. She felt her systems gearing up for a brawl. She'd never liked bullies or braggarts, and the bigger woman fitted both categories. Rosie needed a lesson.

"Come and get it," Sami challenged quietly as she wiped her muddy palms on her navy skirt.

Rosie's laughter ended in a "whoof" as she landed on her stomach in the pit. Sami straddled her and forced Rosie's arm behind her back, pressing it up between the wrestler's shoulderblades. Her fingers tangled in the long muddy hair, forcing Rosie's face down into the slime—just once, for the good of all humanity, she thought as Rosie wriggled free. The Amazon tried to crawl out of the pit, but Sami wanted revenge.

She hiked up her skirt, leaped on Rosie's back, and applied an armlock, her forearm circling the wrestler's neck. "Apologize," she demanded just as two big hands slid beneath her armpits to pry her free.

"Sami," Ben reprimanded from the contours of a bloodied and swollen mouth as he placed her on her feet. "That's enough!"

"Oh . . ." she groaned, frustrated. He *would* interfere, just when Rosie's lesson in manners was going so well! His battered lips attempted a grin, his single open lid allowing the gray eye a maddening twinkle down at her.

Sami did what she had to do. She lifted her palms and thrust them as hard as she could against his chest. His lean backside landed beside Rosie in the mud pit. She dusted her hands and thought how absolutely lovely they looked together. There in the slime. With matching expressions of disbelief.

"Hooray for the champ!" Big hands lifted her to the winner's throne: two lumberjacks' shoulders. "She downed both Ben and Rosie."

Carrying her toward the bar, the men disregarded her plea to please let her down. They seated her on the polished surface and thrust a mug of beer in her hand. "How about a rematch next Saturday night, lady? I didn't have a chance to bet on you tonight," a cowboy asked as he urged the mug to her lips.

The cold malt taste dampened a small percentage of Sami's anger. The sight of Ben, dripping and forging a path toward her, cleared the remainder of her fury. A cowboy slapped a brass belt about her waist and secured it tightly. "Jeez, ma'am. You're small but you're fast. Rosie didn't have a chance," he complimented.

"Move over. Coming through." Ben's curt order turned the men's heads from her. Striding toward her, he was muddy, the buttons torn from his shirt. The heels of her navy shoes protruded from his chest pockets.

When he reached Sami, Ben calmly tossed her over his shoulder and carried her out of the tavern. "Stop your wriggling, woman. Don't you know what it does to men like these?"

"Ben Woden! Let me down!"

"Nope. No telling what you might do." He eased her into the front seat of the Bronco. "Cool off, champ."

"I *am* cool." At least she felt measurably relieved. There was a lot to be said for physical retribution, she admitted to herself. The memory of Ben's shocked expression as he sailed backward into the pit still pleasured her immensely.

"It's cold in here," she observed.

He flipped on the heater. "Of course. We're both covered with mud."

Sami inspected her clothing. The sheer blouse clung to her peaked nipples. "Oh, my goodness!"

"That's why I carried you out, wildcat. I didn't feel like fighting every cowboy who ogled you. George was enough of a fight for one night." He glared at her. "And if you hadn't reacted to Rosie's digs, this whole thing wouldn't have started."

Sami was astonished, not to mention furious. "She wasn't *my* girl friend. I think you're blaming the wrong party."

His "huh" did nothing to soothe her temper. *"You're* wearing the Champion Mud Wrestler belt; I'm not," he accused.

Sami tried to loosen the huge brass buckle, but couldn't budge it. "Is *that* what this is?"

"Damn right. Rosie wants a challenge match next Saturday night."

"But . . . but . . . Oh, my goodness!" Did all the world have to be against her? When did life become so complicated? Ben's grim profile offered no solace.

The Bronco's headlights rose and fell each time the vehicle crossed a deep rut. Sami studied the foliage and, amazed at her own lack of curiosity, said fully, "This isn't the way to your ranch."

His gaze skimmed her disheveled, mud-stained clothing. Long strands of her hair had escaped from the less-than-tidy topknot. "That's right, champ. We both need to clean up before we head back to the house. My line shack is just up the road; we can use it."

The single-room cabin contained a stove, a supply of canned foods, a woodpile, and a cot. It lacked the privacy of a bathroom.

Ben tossed back a canvas tarp to reveal a variety of machines. "This is a portable generator," he explained as he turned the hand crank several times, making the machine whir. He picked up two buckets and started out the door. "Make yourself useful. Roll that galvanized washtub into the corner and throw a blanket over this rope if you want privacy. I'll bring up water from the creek."

Warning bells jangled in Sami's mind. Always volatile, in his present mood, Ben was nothing less than explosive. She looked around the small cabin quickly. Throughout the long, disturbing afternoon and evening, she had wished for the solitude of her room. She badly needed some privacy now, but the log walls, and Ben's presence, seemed to close in on her. She turned to him. "Ah, Ben . . ."

"I'm not in the mood to argue, ma'am." His dark frown was a warning as he strode outside.

Returning moments later, Ben dumped two buckets of water into the tub, glanced at her, and issued a satisfied grunt. He attached a metal coil to the edge of the tub and plugged the electric cord into the generator. "It's a water heater."

He lighted a kerosene heater, adjusted it, and left to fill two more buckets with water. Sami stood, holding her arms protectively before her chest.

Ben returned, again dumped water into the tub, tested its temperature with a swish of his hand, and turned to her. "Get in, champ. It's not the Ritz, but you can make do."

Her fingernails bit into her upper arms. "Ah . . . I'll wait until we get home."

"And have Emma jump all over me for letting you track mud all over her clean house? No, thanks. You undress while I get more water. Toss your clothes on the floor. I'll soak them in the buckets." The fierce line of his brows lowered. "I'm not exactly in a happy mood, you know."

Some moments later, however, Ben's mood changed abruptly when Sami stepped from the shelter of the hanging blanket. Squatting beside the kerosene heater, he was stirring a pot of soup and wishing he hadn't played the part of the jealous husband at the art show.

Sami's small hands clutched the blanket tightly about her as she stepped hesitantly near him.

He wanted to hold her, to erase the memory of the past hours with something that would please her, but instead he continued stirring the soup. "This will be ready in a moment. I swished out your clothes and hung them over the heater to dry. I'm afraid your blouse is ruined."

"Thank you for helping me, Ben." Her voice trembled, and he saw the pale oval of her face staring down at him, her long, damp hair draped about her shoulders. Lord, how he wanted her. Yet he wanted more than sex: He wanted her gentleness wrapped about him. And he wanted to return it, to shelter her with every particle of himself.

Aware of her vulnerability now, and to stay his need of her warmth, Ben stood and stretched. "I could use a little cleaning up, too. Have some soup if you want it, Sami."

He refilled the tub, then undressed behind the hanging blanket and eased down into the water, folding his long legs to fit the small space. George had used body punches, and now Ben's stomach and ribs ached. Several of his bones, broken in rodeo falls and since mended, ached. He swished the washcloth over his face, dabbed it on his aching jaw. He was too old for fights, but somehow he hadn't felt exactly ancient last night in Sami's arms.

Sami. His battered lip throbbed as he smiled. A lady. A champion mud wrestler. A passionate woman beneath her cool veneer. A man's woman if he ever knew one. His woman.

He eased back against the tub, closing his eyes, remembering the soft purr low in her throat as they made love. Sami.

"Ben?" she asked softly, from beyond the curtain of the blanket. "Are you all right? You just groaned."

He wanted her soft hands on him. "George hit me in a few places I can't reach. It's all right."

She reacted as he'd hoped she would. "I could rub them for you," she offered slowly, softly. Holding aside the blanket, she knelt beside him. She was wearing an old shirt he kept at the cabin for emergencies. It was battered and far too big for her, but on Sami it was beautiful. The sleeves were rolled up to her elbows, and he noted with satisfaction that the missing buttons left it open to her waist.

Her palms touched him lightly, hesitated, then firmly flattened on his back. Ben flexed his shoulders. He loved the timid skim of her soft hands over his flesh, the gentle touch of her fingertips. "That feels good, ma'am."

Her hands continued, the strokes firmer, fingertips kneading his taut neck muscles. Ben's eyes closed as he drifted into pleasure. She smoothed his chest, skimming the planes slowly until Ben's hand rose to cover hers. When he eyelids opened, he saw the dark, sensual velvet of her eyes.

"Sami?" he asked huskily. He wanted her, needed her.

"I'm sorry you were hurt, Ben," she answered softly.

She rose, turned, and left him to finish his bath. When he stepped from the enclosure, a towel wrapped about his hips, Sami stood at the single window, hugging herself as she stared into the darkness. The loneliness of her stance and the proud tilt of her head indicated she needed to be left alone, and Ben obliged her. Quietly, he filled his cup with soup, sat on the cot, and leaned back against the wall.

His gaze returned to the long raven sweep of her hair, her squared shoulders beneath the huge shirt, and the bare curves of her legs. He knew Sami was sorting out her thoughts. When she turned slowly, it seemed natural to set the cup on the floor and open his arms to her.

"Come here, little bit." He knew the loneliness in her

expression as though it were his own. He had spent years fighting it. When she glided into his arms, tears slipping down her cheek, he eased her down with him to lie full length on the cot. He tucked the blanket about her gently and sheltered her in his arms, one hand stroking her head.

She nuzzled the hair on his chest, finger-walked through the coarseness as they watched the flames in the kerosene heater. Lord, he thought, she's sweet to the touch. He could lie and just hold her until the town sent out search parties.

He rubbed his cheek against the satin length of her hair, enjoying the fragrance surrounding him. When she stirred restlessly, he tilted her face to his with the tip of his forefinger. "Uncomfortable?"

"You're as big as a moose, Ben Woden," she murmured. "I don't think this cot was made for two."

"Mmm," he agreed, shifting her to lie on top of him. "How's that?"

"You're lumpy and hard in all the wrong places." Sami's lashes flickered over the velvet brown of her eyes. "I don't know how to deal with all this."

"This what?" The softness of her thighs made him ache as they settled over his.

His hands rested lightly on her waist, forced to remain there by a determination that wavered when he realized exactly how full and warm her breasts were against him. He felt the sweat break out on his upper lip as he tried not to think about the very feminine lure of her curves.

"It's as if my world has gone spinning out of orbit and I'm not in control of my life." Her head settled beneath his chin and she sighed. "Sometimes everything is just a little much."

He knew the truth of her statement. The male feelings surging through him as she stirred again were not exactly paternal or brotherly. Her arch stroked his inner calf slowly, adding to his conflicting needs—he wanted to soothe her, but he also wanted to make love to her.

"Ben, you look as though you're in pain. Am I hurting you?" The concern in her expression deepened his conflict.

She looked so trusting that part of him hated the way he manipulated her with his next words. "My lip hurts, that's all." Sami's light kiss on the tender spot ignited a deeper ache, as he'd known it would.

"I detest brawls, Ben. They settle nothing."

"You were pretty feisty tonight, Sami, for a lady."

"I had to oblige. It was a matter of honor. But it won't happen again." She slanted a glance down at him. "At least I'm a champion. Did you win?"

"Of course."

"Bravo." She studied the angles of his face intently. Her finger trailed lightly over the crooked bridge of his nose. "No more whiskey, Ben. And no more fighting."

"All right." In her arms, he'd have agreed to walk over live coals.

Her finger moved across his lashes and down to his lips. It explored first one corner, then the other, before entering his mouth. Around the slender length, Ben whispered hoarsely, "I . . . ah . . . am not used to holding a woman and not making love to her, Sami. You're skating on thin ice."

"Well, I'll be," she whispered before settling her mouth softly over his. When it lifted, she asked, "Did that hurt you?"

"The pain was immense. Kiss it and make it better," Ben ordered. Butterfly light, his palms cupped the soft globes of her breasts.

She drew back. "I'm afraid, Ben," she admitted softly.

He watched the long spiked sweep of her lashes downward. "Why, honey?"

"I'm afraid of my feelings."

"Trust me, Sami."

"For now, Ben, I'd like to"—she gasped as he stroked her palm downward to his stomach—"explore the possibilities . . ."

He chuckled shakily. "Little bit, for now I think we should concentrate on the matter at hand and let tomorrow take care of itself."

"We could concentrate on kissing," Sami suggested teasingly.

"I second the motion," Ben whispered, brushing his lips lightly across the softness of hers. He groaned achingly, settling his mouth on hers with a lover's demand.

- 8 -

THURSDAY MORNING, SAMI'S excited nieces interrupted her warm, fuzzy daydream. She had lost time-spaces all morning, drawn into the memory of Saturday night's lovemaking. Unusual, she thought, very uncharacteristic. But then, when she was with Ben, reality always seemed to slip away.

"Auntie, Mikey wants to take Lori and me swimming in the cottonwood slough," Mary Jane chirped as she entered the study, followed by Ben, with Lori perched on his shoulders.

"Swimming? I thought Mike had a date with Judy this afternoon," Sami said as evenly as she could when Ben's gaze locked with hers.

Mary Jane pouted, and she held her hands behind her denim overalls. "Mikey likes us, too. He's taking us all to the swimming hole, and Emma's frying chicken for our picnic right now." Her big brown eyes narrowed accusingly at her aunt. "It's almost the middle of July, and *somebody* has to take us swimming. If we fell in the ocean, we wouldn't know how to swim and we'd drown."

Sami tugged her one of her niece's braids affectionately. Not only had the children healed from malnourishment and physical and mental abuse, they had developed a healthy measure of self-importance. "It sounds like fun. Am I invited?"

Mary Jane hesitated, shuffling her sandals against the study's hardwood floor, her head averted.

"Ben told her not to let you go," Lori stated imperiously from her perch on his shoulder. "He said he wanted to take you into town to do some shopping while he does some business stuff."

"Hey! You weren't supposed to tell her everything," Ben said as he shifted Lori down to his arms. He leaned against the door frame. His gray eyes darkened as they touched Sami's lips. Despite their lovemaking, Sami was not comfortable in the same room with him. He was too masculine, too aware of how distressing he was to her system. The smoky gaze stalked her each time she turned, ringing an alarm that sent her running in the opposite direction.

"Have you told them about winning your belt yet?"

"Ben!"

"Auntie? What belt?"

Ben placed Lori on her feet. He walked toward Sami in a glide of broad shoulders, narrow hips, and long-legged jeans. He smelled of pine trees and sun, and Sami's heart contracted as he smiled down at her. "Ma'am?"

The intimate rumble of his voice caused her fingers to tremble. She placed the book she was holding on the desk. The weakness in her knees forced her to sit before she crumpled. There was no doubt that Ben caused major earthquakes on the floor beneath her feet when he looked at her.

"Auntie, what belt?" Lori insisted.

Ben hooked his thumbs in his waistband and tilted

his head to the angle that said explain-yourself-out-of-this-one. He leaned back against the book-lined shelves.

When she glowered at him, he shrugged. "Everybody's talking about it, Sami. Rosie wants a rematch."

"Rosie?" chorused both girls. "Rematch?"

"Girls, I'll tell you all about it after you've gone swimming, okay? You'd better hurry and tell Mike you want to go."

Distracted from their questions, the girls ran to find Mike.

Sami did not like the rancher's confident smile. Much too masculine, too many white teeth showing. She felt like Little Red Riding Hood tripping down the path to where the wolf lay in wait for her. She didn't want to ask his help, but she was forced to. "Ben, you've got to help me out of this mess."

He pushed away from the bookcase. This morning, Ben resembled a pirate, Sami decided. The sable lock crossing his brow and the sensuality of his stare completed the picture. She felt much like the swashbuckler's captive princess as he continued to stare at her intently.

He sat on the corner of the desk. "You're been avoiding me since Sunday. That's four days of bruised ego," he calculated.

He was concerned about his ego? Sami's problem was Rosie, the Hun. "All this . . . wrestling is your fault," she accused. She began to feel tiny starbursts of anger. "*You* took me to Fred's Diner. *You* touched Rosie and made George mad."

"Honey, you didn't just protect yourself. They've got you billed as 'The Wyoming Wildwoman.'"

Sami jumped to her feet, pacing back and forth as her agitation erupted. "This is horrible, just grotesque. I have a master's degree in education. I like Bach, Beethoven, Chopin. I'm the guardian of two precious little girls, for goodness' sake."

Her hands slashed the air as she expanded. "All my life, I've tried to be a gentle person. A lady, if you will." She rounded on him, arms akimbo. "Ben, you've got to get me out of this," she demanded.

He chafed his jaw with the flat of his hand. Despite Sami's irritation, she noted the change in Ben since she had first met him. His lean cheeks were always shaved now, his eyes clear in the mornings, free of hangover redness. His humor was almost boyish, his grizzly-bear moods spaced further apart.

"Ben?" she prompted.

"It will cost you," he drawled softly. "The Wyoming Wildwoman already has bets placed on her. I'll have to think about it."

"I do not intend to brawl at Fred's Diner!" Sami exploded. "Do something!"

"Hmmm." His brown index finger stroked the bridge of his nose as he thought. Somehow Sami found the small crook in the otherwise perfect line quite . . . lovable. Like a comfortable pair of worn high-heels shoes. She shook her head, trying to clear it of Ben's endearing habits. Like the way his head tilted when he listened intently to a new idea.

But then the image of Rosie, angered and ready for a rematch, flashed before her. Rosie had a reputation to protect . . . while Sami had bones and flesh to protect. "I'll do anything," she promised wildly as he stroked his nose once more.

"I thought you'd see it my way, ma'am. I want you to go into town with me. I have some business at the bank that will require your signature; then we'll do some shopping . . ." He shrugged a very wide set of shoulders.

"What kind of business would require my signature, Ben?"

The confident, wolfish gleam changed into a veiled wariness. He took a deep breath, held it before exhaling slowly. "I set up trust funds for Lori and Mary Jane."

"You *what?*" Surely, those well-molded lips had not

said what Sami's ears had just heard. She looked at them more closely as Ben repeated the sentence.

"Both girls will need trust funds. As their guardian, you'll have to sign the papers."

"I think you're overstepping the bounds of our relationship, Ben." She didn't want or need his charity. Once she landed a teaching job at a school, she would be able to support the children and establish savings accounts for them. Ben Woden had stuck his big boot in where it didn't belong. He was hard enough to deal with already. She didn't want to be indebted to him, too.

He sighed. "I thought you might take it that way, honey. But the banker has all the papers ready. I like those kids, and they need some security."

"You could have asked."

"Why? I was going to do it anyway."

"Ben, you are an exasperating person."

Sami Lassiter had her back up, Ben decided at two o'clock that afternoon as he parked on the street in front of the bank and surveyed the pin-striped pants suit, white blouse, and black pumps, and the tightly pinned topknot. She had answered his attempts at conversation with all the liveliness of a belly-up trout. Well, he amended silently, Sami couldn't be compared to a dead fish. Not under any circumstances. She kept a man on his toes, alternately playing the genteel lady and the wary, vulnerable woman-child. And he wanted more than the white-hot passion between them. But how to get it?

He tried smiling down at her as they entered the bank. His smiled died, unreturned. He attempted another one as the banker completed the transaction, and again when Sami signed her flowing signature. Her brown eyes regarded him coolly from behind the tinted lenses, as though he had never entered her life, never made love to her. He wanted her in his life—permanently, dammit.

"Okay," he erupted as he reversed the Bronco and jammed it into forward gear. "I made a mistake. I should have asked you about the trust accounts. I'm just not used to having to ask anyone about anything, I guess."

Her "humph" of disbelief challenged him.

"Okay," he added, slashing a glance at her arms, crossed rigidly over her chest. "It's done now. What would make you happy about it?"

"I earn my keep, Mr. Woden," she stated disdainfully. "It has to do with pride."

Women had all sorts of little intricacies to their thinking processes, he decided. "Hell, I like those kids. I just wanted to do something for their future, that's all," he stated finally. "You're acting as if I'd committed grand larceny. If you want to earn their gifts, I'll think of something, but it's not necessary. To me, at least."

He saw the flicker of satisfaction in her eyes before she lowered her incredibly long, silky, black lashes. He remembered the feel of them against his cheek. "Am I free of Rosie the Hun now?" she asked softly.

His belly contracted. Free. That's what Sami really wanted. To be free, to lead her own well-planned life without him. He felt a cold shudder tingle down his spine. For one of the few times in his life, Ben experienced fear. He knew he had to keep her warmth.

At that moment Ben decided he would work his backside off to keep Sami. She wanted conversation; he'd give her conversation. She liked fine foods; he could swallow something other than steak, no matter how small, how disgusting. She was educated and . . . well, he'd have to work on that one. Shoot.

". . . Rosie? Mud wrestling?" Sami prompted. He glanced at her tilted-up nose, eyes a man could drown in, and the sweetness of her rosebud lips. He wanted her as he had never wanted anything or anyone in forty-one years. And there was one thing an old mountain trapper like him knew: You have to use bait the quarry wants.

"I'm working it out. I just don't have all the angles covered yet."

"Ben!"

He looked at her, pulling out what would have to be his most charming smile. "I do some of my best thinking after a good meal. We could stop here in town."

"I refuse to go to Fred's Diner."

"Okay. There's a nice place outside the city limits." Actually, he preferred Fred's. The restaurant he'd suggested was too quiet, known for its French cuisine. "I'll call and reserve a table while we're shopping."

A half-hour later, Sami was furious. Anger caused her stomach to knot and her fingertips to tremble. She had agreed to go into the ladies' clothing store and had let Ben lead her to an isolated nook lined with mirrors. But she would not agree to let him purchase a dress for her. Especially the one dangling from the crook of his finger. "No, thank you. No," she added more firmly.

He dangled the garment over his long arm, inspecting the flowing pink lines. "What's wrong with it?" Eyebrows drawn into a single line, he studied the dress intently. "Wrong size?"

"It's the right size! But I don't like the idea of you buying me clothing."

Ben stared down at her face. "I have some heavy thinking to do. Everyone is all revved up about Rosie's rematch, and it's going to take a mastermind to get you out of this mess. And it's damned difficult when you're wearing that." His large hand swept downward, palm up.

"It's a basic pin-striped business suit," she protested. "You're wearing one too. I fail to see the difference." Ben wore his clothing well. His navy suit fitted his broad shoulders and long legs snugly. A subdued silk tie complemented his light blue shirt.

He cupped her shoulder with his palm, turned her to

face the full-length mirror. "Look. You look like a half-grown boy. We've got to change your image so I can get you out of your mud-wrestling career. You need to appear as if you never wallowed in it." He ignored her glare. "Now, look." He held the dress in front of her and the pink fabric settled softly against her.

But Sami stared at his reflection, as he stood behind her. There was an eagerness in the craggy lines of his face. He looked like a child expectantly awaiting his Christmas presents. Beneath his thick lashes, his eyes glittered, and his fingers trembled as he caressed her neck.

Enthralled by the smoky gaze, Sami did not object as his forearm pressed her chest, urged her back against his hard, warm body. His eyes held hers as his lips tasted the smoothness of her temples, then trailed down the side of her cheek. "You're very desirable, Sami. You take my breath away."

The husky baritone plucked strings inside her; golden mists tingled warmly down her lower stomach and legs. It was difficult to think when Ben's warm breath swirled in her ear, when the slight roughness of his cheek slid up and down on hers.

"Dearling," he whispered. His lips brushed her skin leaving it warm and flushed.

"Dearling?" she asked. Her nervous system settled into a layer of clouds as he repeated the word.

"I read it in a novel about ladies and knights. It suits you, Sami." The reflection of Ben's stare held hers. "An endearing little creature smelling of sweet grass and bluebells."

She pushed a swallow down her dry throat. Against her spine, Ben's chest rumbled as he spoke. The words were spoken slowly, and she knew they were unrehearsed. Ben's personality did not lend itself to the lyrical; he was a blunt-spoken man. She knew he was an honorable man who loved his son, who cared deeply for those around him. Yet he reminded her of a mountain cat circling his prey, cunning and determined.

And he was entirely too close to her. She melted more quickly each time he touched her. She concentrated on the reflection of his face. *It*—the hunter in pursuit—lurked there, beneath the hard bones and tanned flesh and smoky eyes.

Ben wanted too much from her. She scanned the dark hair waving over his brow, the width of his body behind hers, then moved away, her knees threatening to buckle. He wanted to win more than the sensual war, and she couldn't afford to let him have the victory. Her letters to schools had been answered; several interviews for teaching positions were scheduled within the month. In another month, she and the girls would leave the ranch. It was better to keep Ben on the perimeter of her emotions. *If she could.*

Lose the battle, win the war, she thought. She took the dress from the crook of his finger, avoiding his stare. "I'll try this on."

Ben Woden was extremely pleased with himself. He grinned only too easily, Sami thought. During their meal, she excused the press of his knees and calves down the length of hers; after all, his long legs ill fitted the small restaurant table. And she excused the way he casually draped his arm across the back of her chair. After all, there was just too much of him for the Chez Marie furniture.

Sami smiled when he ordered a Bordeaux wine for them. She admired his determination to enjoy the fondue au fromage, artichauts à la greque, and tournedos. Ben acted every inch the country squire. He was charming, attentive, and at ease on the trip home, until she asked, "What are you planning to do about Rosie?"

"What about Rosie?"

Sami stared at him. "The papers. The dress. My new

image," she reminded him. "This." Ben had insisted she wear her hair free, and she lifted a lock.

"I'm still thinking. Let's talk about it while we eat." He parked the Bronco in front of a combination lounge and restaurant.

"We just ate, Ben."

"Huh. I need real food. Emma doesn't like me rummaging through her kitchen at night. Besides I'm still working on your new image." He crossed in front of the vehicle and opened her door.

Sami planted her shoes on the floorboard and her back against the seat, and glared at him. He couldn't be trusted. Prince Charming had vanished, his tie gone, his shirt unbuttoned. Now he reminded her of . . . a wrestling trainer.

He slid his big hand beneath the one she had braced against the upholstery. "I can't think on an empty stomach."

Why me? Sami thought a few minutes later as she watched him wolf down an inch-thick steak and a side platter of french fires.

She nibbled on a cracker and sipped a glass of water. The booth seemed undersized with Ben in it next to her. He was just too . . . confident for her taste. The evening up to this point had been palatable, but Ben was stalling now. She felt it in her bones. He had that I've-got-her-where-I-want-her look written all over him, and it grated.

"I'll have a beer." The white teeth gleamed in the neon light as he smiled down at her. "What do you want to drink, Sami? White wine?"

Ordinarily, wine would have been her choice, but now she felt like rebelling. Ben's smile widened. He thought he knew her and held her right in his big callused palm. "I'd like something stronger, please."

Ben's eyebrows went up. She rather liked the surprise written on his tanned face. "The bartender mixed up a batch of Fuzzy Navels," the waitress offered. "They're really good."

"Fine. I'd like one, please." It didn't matter what she drank. It was worth any price to see Ben's incredulous expression.

The first glass of orange juice and peach schnapps was delicious down to the last piece of crushed ice. And the second Fuzzy Navel tasted better than the first. Sami felt fuzzy herself around the edges. Warm. Nice. Just right to be cuddled.

She located Ben's amused face in the imaginary camera lens formed by the tips of her index fingers and her thumbs. He winked at her when she tried to zoom in.

"I think we'd better go home now, Sami." He caught her hands in his and held them on the table. She examined the broad backs of his hands, his strong fingers, and neatly clipped nails, then turned his palms upward. She traced the callused mounds and lifeline with the tip of her forefinger and heard his inhaled breath.

Sami was a dangerous woman, Ben decided. Every curvaceous ounce of her could put a man through his paces if ever she wanted to, and the erotic slide of her fingertip over his flesh was noticeably affecting some male areas of his physique.

The silky length of her lashes slowly lowered. "Do you know I've never necked?" Her eyes opened. "Have you?"

Ben's body hardened even more. He wasn't too certain who was in control of the moment, the cowboy or the lady. He was oddly uncomfortable as she continued to stare at him. Sami's expression was purely female invitation. The tip of her tongue trailed across her bottom lip, moistening it. Damn, Ben thought. He even felt a little shy.

"I parked a few times in my youth." Perspiration cooled his upper lip. He wiped it away with the back of his hand as though it were beer foam. Cords tightened down the length of his body. He *had* been in control of the game plan, Ben thought dazedly. But somehow, Sami had turned the tables on him.

"Old man." She smiled slowly, the tilt of her head slanting a long wave down the satiny flush of her cheek. "Probably too old."

Sami was flirting with him. Her soft Arkansas drawl tantalized his insides, destroyed his good intentions to woo her as a lady. God help him if she ever discovered the true extent of her power over him.

"I probably imagined the other night," she teased.

Inexperienced or not, sober or saturated with Fuzzy Navels up to her beautiful eyeballs, Sami could tie him in knots. He could almost feel the natural flow of her body beneath him. Hell, how much could a man take?

"You didn't dream the other night. I'm your lover."

"In Arkansas, they'd say you're my man." Her soft palm slid over his, her slender fingers lacing with his strong ones. "I still respect you, Ben."

"Just so you don't think I'm easy."

Her eyes widened. "Never that, Ben. I've always respected you, even when you act like an old grizzly. But you do make me so mad sometimes. Like today. You know you should have asked me about the girls' trust accounts," she chastised.

The words were rusty and old. He'd never spoken them before. They came hard: "I'm sorry, little bit."

"You must consult me about things as important as this, Ben."

"Yes, little bit."

"I've never parked in my life, and I want to learn now, Ben."

"Yes, Sami."

"Dad, what time did you get in last night?" Mike asked his father over the breakfast table.

"Isn't that my line, Mike?" Uncomfortable, Ben shifted in his chair, jabbing the scrambled eggs with his fork. Damn. Emma, Dan, and Mike all stared steadily at him. At his feet, Chug's baleful brown eyes condemned him. Mary Jane and Lori, seated on his lap, smiled up at him, unaware of the silent accusations passing over their heads.

"Sami Lassiter is a fine woman." Dan's statement lashed over the table. "Don't want nothin' to hurt her."

Mary Jane examined a scar on Ben's jaw with her fingertip. "Auntie's still sleeping," she said, innocently punctuating the condemnation.

"Despoiler of the innocent. Womanizer," Emma's harsh whisper censured. "I don't suppose you have good intentions toward the girl. And she having such a hard time of it, too. Come on, Dan. Let's you and me and the girls go check the garden for gophers." Emma lowered her wooden spoon in front of Ben's nose. "You talk to your pa, Mike. But good."

After they had gone, Mike leaned back in his chair and crossed his arms over his chest. "You're in the doghouse, Dad," he said mildly.

Ben sipped his coffee. He was a grown man, sitting in his own house. Yet, under Mike's steady gaze, he felt like a convict standing before a judge. He shrugged.

"This is the big time, Dad," Mike continued "What's the story between you and Sami? And don't tell me it isn't any of my business. I like her."

"I like her, too."

"How much, Dad? Enough to play games, or enough to marry her? She's a lady, Dad. I don't think she understands a lot of things."

Ben looked at his son. Mike was no longer a glib high school dropout. Under Sami's tutelage, he had become a young man, determined to enter the world beyond the ranch. Ben leaned back in his chair and met his son's gaze squarely. "Ready for a man-to-man talk, son?"

Mike smiled. "I'm past the birds and the bees stage, Dad."

"I thought I was, too, Mike. But she's knocked me for a loop. The old rules don't apply anymore."

"Life moves on." Mike was clearly biting back a grin. "You're just like the creaky old barn door that needed oiling. You'll get the hang of it. Say nice things. Judy likes that." He shrugged. "I got a whopper of a kiss the other day just for bringing her some daisies and bluebells. Worked like a charm."

"Sami's independent, Mike. Every time I try to do something nice, it backfires." He frowned, then voiced the thought that had been worrying him. "Do you think I'm too old for her?"

"Nah. You're pretty well preserved."

Ben's grin was wry. "Thanks. Then there's the education gap."

Mike placed his hands behind his head. "Tell me about it. I'm right in the middle of that one."

"She wouldn't be content to live on a ranch. She likes concerts, fine food . . ."

"So? You can learn. What's the problem?" Mike asked. "She's a lady, Dad. You're just going to have to put out a little effort to keep her. You're not letting her go, are you? I mean, how many guys have got a pretty tutor who can beat big Rosie in mud-wrestling? She's a real find."

Ben remembered her snuggling on his lap as he drove home last night. Sated and sweet and slightly tipsy, she had wanted to pull behind the barn and . . .

"She's a hell of a woman," Ben agreed. "When did you get so smart, son?"

"I inherited it, Dad. No charge for the advice. Come to me with your problems anytime."

Sami was cold. Something big and warm pressed down on her stomach, soothing its rocking contents. She forced her lids open, then quickly closed them. "Ben, I'm so cold. My head hurts."

"You're cold, honey, because you have an ice pack on your head. Your head hurts because you aren't used to Fuzzy Navels, and you had two," Ben soothed as he lifted the pack. Sami's frown hurt; her head felt strangely disassembled from the rest of her body. She pried open one eyelid and whispered, "I am not drunk. I never drink. I think the fondue was too rich."

"Okay. But take these aspirins anyway." He lifted her head and held the glass of water to her lips. "That's a good girl, little bit."

"It must be a virus. I'll just rest awhile."

"Do you think you could move over? I'd like to hold you." Sami's eyelids opened. Above her, Ben tenderly smiled. She was too tired to wonder about the softness etched in his expression, and she did want to have his arms about her. Maybe they would make the rocking motion stop. Ben had such strong arms.

"Have you thought of a plan yet?" she asked after he fitted his long length behind her. "For Rosie?"

He nuzzled the tender spot behind her ear, his arms sliding around her. His palm cupped her breast gently, warmly. "Uh-huh. This morning I arranged for two professionals to wrestle at Fred's. Rosie will challenge the winner. They're stealing your thunder, ma'am. The Wyoming Wildwoman has just retired."

"Thank you, Ben." She snuggled closer to the warm cove his lap made at the back of her thighs. Ben was an extremely comfortably padded man. She liked him. Last night, he'd grumbled a little about the cramped space and the steering wheel as he taught her how to neck. But he had laughed, too. And he had saved her from Rosie. "What time is it?" Reality began to creep softly about her.

"About ten. Everyone else is up and outside the house. How are you feeling now?" He nibbled her earlobe, then tickled it with his tongue.

"Stop that. I'm feeling much better, thank you."

"Cozy?"

She shifted her head on his well-padded arm, nodding. "Yes, thank you."

"Not mad at me anymore about the girls' trust accounts?"

The length of Sami's body tightened beneath the quilts. "I'm enormously angry with you concerning that."

"We can't have the Wyoming Wildwoman angry, ma'am. Whoof . . ." She jabbed her elbow into his flat stomach. Revenge *is* sweet, Sami decided before his arms tightened about her.

"What do you think about tutoring me for the GED, Sami?" he asked suddenly. "It would be double duty. It's difficult to stuff an old cowboy's head, you know. Probably a lot more difficult than working with Mike. But you'd be earning the girls' accounts, and you seem to feel you should do that."

She heard the tremor in his deep voice and knew his uncertainty. A man with Ben's pride could be a difficult student. "Well, what do you think about the idea, little bit? We'd both be getting something out of the deal."

She turned to face him. "Why are you rubbing my stomach?" The dark flush crept up from his collar, but his expression was desolate. He avoided her eyes.

"Just to keep it from growling, honey." His hand slid around her waist and rested on the jut of her hip. "You're awfully pretty, little bit. Young and tender, sweet right down to your toes. I'd like to get educated by you."

When Ben's voice dropped to that pleasing rumble, Sami's mental processes went on strike. "Judging by the way you run your businesses, and the books in the study, you could probably pass the tests without even trying. I have some canvases ready to frame. By the end of the summer, I could pay a portion of the trusts back—"

His finger prowled the bow-shaped curve of her upper lip.

"But I've always wanted to graduate from high school. You could make my dream come true."

Sami leaned back in the circle of his arm. "Somehow I distrust the sound of that statement."

Ben grinned lazily and stretched, yawning. "A man could get used to your soft ways, woman. I think I could lie here all day."

"You take up too much room."

"Do I have a deal, sweetheart? Will you tutor me as well as Mike?"

"Of course. I'm sure you'll be as good a student as Mike, and he's doing well. All I have to do now is point him in the right direction and he passes the chapter tests with flying colors. In fact, I've been working with him in the mornings and painting in the afternoons. Let's see, it's mid-July now . . . Yes, he'll pass his exams in early August."

"Well, just point me in the right direction. When do we start?"

"I'd like to start today, right after lunch. Mike is working on a report, and I'll have time then."

"Fine. I'll be there."

Children's voices called downstairs. "Ben, please . . ." Sami's plea was silenced by Ben's mouth over hers.

"Kiss me, little bit. Or I won't leave."

A half-hour after lunch, Sami ran in front of the Bronco. She placed her hands on her hips and spread her jeaned legs apart. Just two yards from her, Ben jammed on the brakes, killed the engine, and jumped out of the vehicle. He stalked toward her.

"What the hell are you doing, Sami? I might not have been able to stop in time." He matched her stance, arms akimbo, long legs spread wide, his dusty boots firmly planted. His eyebrows joined, matching the pugnacious set of his jaw. "Okay, what did I do now? Spit it out. You look like you're going to explode."

"Mr. Woden, it's past time for your classes. You were to meet me in the study at one o'clock for testing."

He stared down at her, and his jaw moved as he gritted his teeth. "I told you at lunch it would have to wait. There's a livestock sale at the Johnsons'. I want those blooded Limousin heifers for the Baron."

Sami tapped her canvas-shod toe and crossed her arms over her chest. "I see. You make promises you don't keep."

His face darkened thunderously beneath the battered straw hat. "Now, Sami," he growled. "I'm not in a mood—"

"Oh, I see. It is Mr. Ben Woden's moods we must protect today. He can play truant while the rest of us mortals must deal with everyday problems of life."

Ben's wide shoulders tensed, ridging the chambray material covering them. When he spoke, the sound raised the fine hairs on the back of Sami's neck. "I don't think I like the sound of that, woman."

He loomed over her, his shadow blocking out the July noon sun. "I said I'd take your damn tests. But this is important."

"Importance is where you place it, Ben," Sami stated flatly. "I have a job to do, and it's important to me."

"You're feeling pretty feisty now, aren't you, half-pint?" The slate-gray eyes heated Sami's flesh beneath her cotton T-shirt and jeans. The sensual gaze caused her stomach to tighten, while her bones felt as if they had all the strength of a noodle. His eyes rested on the single braid draped across her left breast.

One black brow arced as he stared down at her. His mood shifted subtly, she decided, into lazy indulgence. "It's too pretty a day to spend inside, Sami. You could come with me. It's a beautiful drive to the Johnson ranch."

She had to be firm. It didn't matter that her heart tried to thud out of her chest when his head tilted down at her that way. It didn't matter that her stomach knotted when the right corner of his mouth sloped upward. Ben had the word *hunter* written all over his very sexy stance. She didn't trust him. Just being close to him had all the impact of five Fuzzy Navels. She sensed him circling her mentally, probing into personal areas of her being. When he did that, he made her nervous. "Either you want to pass your GED or you don't. I can paint instead of teaching you this afternoon," she erupted.

"Of course I want to pass it. Truly, I do," he drawled easily.

"What are you up to, Ben?" Sami cocked her head to one side. He was her lover now, but when the summer ended . . . she could not afford a deeper entanglement.

But behind those smoke gray eyes a schemer stalked her.

Her nieces' laughter erupted from the playground, and Ben glanced at the girls, then back down at her. "Have you ever thought about raising your own babies, Sami?" he asked softly.

- 9 -

"I'M YOUR MAN, honey. You're my woman. You've got skin that feels like cream under my hands, you wear cotton underpants, and you'd fight the Baron for your ideals. And you sure as hell have all the right equipment to be a mother," Ben continued.

Sami stared up at Ben's rawboned face. Fighting the wild flush crawling up her neck, she pressed her trembling fingertips against her thighs. "You're crude, Ben Woden. Downright crude."

His expression closed, muscles shifting in the corded neck, his eyes glittering between the veil of black lashes. His hard mouth tightened as he matched her stare.

He shifted his stance, hooking a thumb into his leather belt. He tilted his straw hat against the brightness of the sun. "Could be. But you've got me wound around your little finger, honey. And that gives me certain rights."

Sami's small hands shot out, palms upward. Ben was

the most frustrating man she knew. He was pushing; she didn't like it. "No one asked you for anything. You have no rights over me. None." She slashed the air before his face.

Ben snaked out a big hand, wrapped it about her wrists, and drew her palms to his mouth. His other arm wrapped around her waist to draw her against his body. He held her tightly, the span of his hand curving over the roundness of her hip. Locked against him, Sami barely breathed. She was reminded, almost painfully, of the way her softness meshed perfectly with his masculine planes. Ben trembled, his thighs hardening against her.

"Ben! Let me go!" Sami cried as the flat of his hand lowered, pressing her hips into his rigid thighs. Despite her anger, her body softened, the sensual warmth beginning to surge through her. Watching her, he kissed her palm, gently nipped the pad of her thumb with his teeth.

Sami groaned softly, oblivious of the noon heat on her shoulders and the children's curious eyes. She was aware only of the desire growing low in her stomach.

"What are you going to do with all this, Sami?" Huskily, he added, "You're like a furnace in my arms now. And propinquity has nothing to do with it, honey. You feel something deep inside, and you're working like hell to bury it. You don't want to be committed to a cowboy who doesn't know Bach from Brahms."

Dry-throated, mesmerized by the stark pain of his expression, Sami whispered, "I don't know what you're talking about." But she could not meet his accusing stare, and lowered her lashes as tears threatened to flow.

"I want you, dammit!" he cursed. "More than that. How many times do you think a man and a woman experience what we have? The passion and sharing of pain. Pride and laughter. Damn seldom. Life's too cold, Sami. You've been there, and so have I. I want to make a new life for us. I won't let you turn your back on it."

Sami's eyelids opened to the full blast of his darkly

flushed face. A muscle jerked on his cheekbone; his eyes were suspiciously bright. His uneven breath swept over her face. "I want a commitment, precious. The man-and-woman kind that lasts a lifetime. There was a reason you gave yourself to me. What was it?"

When she couldn't speak, he shook her gently and continued. "Wake up, honey. We can work it out." His big palm framed the fine bones of her face. His thumb caressed the satiny texture slowly, back and forth. "I wouldn't hurt you, Sami. I never will," he promised tautly before releasing her and striding toward the Bronco.

Stunned, Sami trembled, missing the warmth of his body. Ben's silvery gaze locked with hers as he drove near her and hit the brakes. "The postman on our rural route said we needed a larger box for all the correspondence from high schools, and Mike sure as hell isn't applying to them. Don't send out any more of those damned letters applying for teaching jobs, Sami. Things aren't settled between us, and all those letters make me mad as hell," he ground out before driving off in a cloud of Wyoming dust.

During the first week of August, Mike passed his tests and was excited about completing college applications. That same week, Sami interviewed for two teaching positions in nearby schools, and returned home with "We'll let you know soon" responses. She continued her last-minute applications for jobs. She also lost weight and couldn't sleep soundly.

Stoically, Ben listened as Sami explained English grammar, his singular weakness. He grumbled, but completed his assignments neatly and flawlessly. Ben wrote simply, but the depth of his insights stunned Sami; obviously, he had labored over his papers. But he grew lean and taut as a caged mountain lion without a proper diet. Fatigue deepened the lines in his face; the intensity of his eyes when he looked at her was startling, hungry.

One day that same week, Banjo McGee dropped several college catalogs on the breakfast table. "Here's the stuff you asked for, Sami. Every damn thing I could find on Wyoming colleges." He plopped down on a chair and forked four pancakes onto his plate, buttered and poured syrup over them, then added bacon and eggs.

Around a huge mouthful of Emma's pancakes, he murmured, "The land purchase papers for the new condo in Cheyenne need your signature for finalization, Ben. I looked the site over when I flew in from Casper. It cost a pretty piece, but we'll make money on it. We got a contract for prefab homes, and we're gonna need a new timber mill and equipment. I've already talked to accounting—"

Ben leaned back, balancing his chair on two legs. Arms crossed over his chest, brows lowered into a single black line, he glared at Sami's averted head. "Why did you want information on Wyoming colleges, Ms. Lassiter? Are you applying for a job as a professor?" he asked in a tone as cold as the approaching winter nights.

Banjo's red curls seemed to shoot straight out from his head; his blue eyes were alert, darting between Ben's dark expression and the top of Sami's neatly coiled hair. "Hey, Ben. What's the problem? Sami is helping Judy Thacker and Mike with their application forms for colleges. Judy's already been accepted into one college, but she may change if Mike decides on another one, so they can go together. From what I hear, Mike needs a school with a strong art department. He's applying late as it is, and Sami's doing a lot of paperwork and making phone calls to give the kids the best breaks. I thought you knew all that."

Sami pushed her scrambled eggs around the blue china plate. She hadn't wanted breakfast, but Emma insisted that she eat something each morning, acting offended if Sami tried to excuse herself.

Ben was surly and didn't bother to hide it. His words were few, but his eyes glittered savagely beneath the craggy line of his brows, his jaw jutting as pugnaciously as when Sami had first met him. He watched every mouthful she ate at every meal. His mouth became a hard, cruel line when he looked at her, unlike the lazy grin he bestowed on Lori and Mary Jane. She noted the uneasy way he rubbed his lean stomach as if he had an ulcer, and she took note of the half-empty bottle of antacid tablets in the medicine cabinet.

Footsteps padded beyond her closed bedroom door at night. The sound of Ben's indistinct, soothing murmur to Chug slammed her heart against her ribs.

Despite his silent accusations and endless energy, Ben's large, dark hands trembled as they passed near hers over the dinner table, as though he wanted to lace her slender fingers within the dark strength of his. As though he fought that urge.

One late night, she lay still as he cracked her bedroom door. "Move over, Chug, and stop growling," he had whispered to the dog lying in front of her door. "I won't even wake her."

Closing the door, he had padded across the room to stand beside her bed. She could smell the clean soap and the earthy musk rising from his body as his large hand fitted lightly over her head. Gently, he had eased himself down to lie beside her. Behind her, she had heard his long sigh as he placed his arm over her. "Damn you, woman, I need you," he whispered roughly. Moments later, his deep breathing indicated he was asleep.

Sami hadn't cared about his cursing, she only knew she was glad he was there. She had snuggled back against him. In the morning, he was gone, and she wondered if he had really come to her.

Now Banjo's alert eyes locked with hers, then shifted

to Ben's unrelenting gray ones. "I asked what's up? Why are you so jumpy, old buddy?"

"Ms. Lassiter has been applying for jobs everywhere. She's leaving as soon as she gets a good offer." Ben's clipped accusation clawed at Sami's nerves. She let her fork fall to her plate. She had every right to apply and interview. Ben had hired her for the summer only, but he talked as if she were a rat deserting a sinking ship. She wanted to kick his chair legs out from under him and send him sprawling at her feet. Instead, she patted the smooth coil of hair and adjusted the frilly lace collar of her yellow blouse with shaking fingers. "Breakfast was good, Emma. I'm just not very hungry today."

For good measure, she glared at Ben. "If you'll excuse me, I think I'll go study these catalogs now. And I have some business letters to type." Her stomach, beneath the straight yellow skirt, growled loudly, and she pressed the flat of her hand over it.

"Humph! You *never* eat lately," Emma grumbled. "These two," she told Banjo. "One won't eat, and the other one's babying an ulcer."

Banjo laughed. "Sounds like you'd better chow down and skip the paperwork, Sami."

Ben scowled. "Some people eat all the time when they're upset. Sami is just the opposite. She doesn't eat enough to keep a bird alive."

Sami glared at him. "Now, why would I be upset? No one could eat with you snarling all the time. You had no right to tell me to stop applying for jobs," she burst out.

"Hell! You didn't listen to me, did you?" he returned.

She clamped her lips together, refusing to enter a shouting match with him. Why, oh, why, did that man torment her? She'd sidestepped his ornery ways for two weeks, done her business day to day as she should have, and every meal he sat there counting the spoonfuls of food entering her mouth. He was rude. She said as much.

Beside her, Dan cleared his throat and turned to Lori and Mary Jane, who had been watching the adults with round-eyed fascination. "Come on, kids. Emma and me want to show you the new gopher runs by the clothesline. Chug, you, too."

"I'm staying," Banjo announced. "This looks too good to miss."

"Suit yourself," Dan said. "They can get to be just like two fighting cocks squaring off in a ring. They've been arguing since Sami got here."

The front legs of Ben's chair thudded on the kitchen floor just as the screen door closed behind the elderly couple and the children. "My bet's on Sami," Dan whispered over his shoulder. "Let me know how it comes out, Banjo."

Banjo gave him a high sign, touching the tip of his index finger to his thumb.

"You know why I'm rude, Ms. Lassiter. You're driving me crazy!" Ben stated in a low growl.

"I don't have to drive you; you're already there, Mr. Woden," she shot back, unafraid of his darkening scowl.

"I know where I'd like to be, Ms. Lassiter." His eyes narrowed across the table at her, and Sami caught the sensual insinuation. Ben wanted to haul her upstairs and love the living daylights out of her. He wanted her to commit herself to him.

A pang of uneasiness shot through Sami's anger. She felt cornered. Her stomach rumbled loudly—a very unladylike sound. "You're not giving me any space, Ben. I don't like it."

"Hell, woman. I've given you everything I've got, and I'm ready to give more. You're the one who's stubborn."

"Whew!" Banjo whispered from the side arena, his eyes darting from one antagonist to the other as he crammed another forkful of pancake into his mouth.

Ben flicked a glance at his Hawaiian-shirted business manager. "I suppose you're on her side. You're a ball of fluff where women are concerned."

"Oh! Oh!" Sami stammered angrily, rising from her chair. A wave of dizziness washed over her, and she sank back down on the chair weakly.

She heard Ben's chair scrape, followed by the sound of running water; then he knelt beside her. He held her chin in one hand and dabbed a cold, wet washcloth over her face gently. His cool fingers trembled against her hot flesh as he kissed her brow.

Sami was too weak to do anything but stare at the tenderness written on his face. He trailed a hard fingertip over her soft, trembling lips. "Fighting me or not, honey, you have to eat more."

"Wow!" Banjo breathed somewhere beyond Sami's view.

Ben patted the cold cloth across Sami's forehead and gently pressed it to the back of her neck. "Feeling better, honey?" Without waiting for her answer, he said, "I'm taking her upstairs, Banjo."

Sami didn't know what she felt as Ben carried her upstairs and deposited her on the brass bed. He sat beside her, tenderly loosening her clothing. His fingers clumsily unraveled the coil of her hair and lovingly arranged the black tresses about the violet-sprigged pillowcase.

His expression softened for the first time in two weeks. He eased a tendril behind her ear with his index finger, then teased her pearl stud earring. He investigated the fastening behind her earlobe, frowned, and said, "Those damn things look dangerous, honey. They could cut you. I'm taking them out."

Sami caught his broad wrist with both her hands, pushing it from her. "Don't, Ben."

He turned his hand, holding hers lightly. The sad cast to his dark face tore at Sami's unsettled nerves. "When are you going to face it, Sami? Or are you just going to run away from me?"

He sighed. The heavily indrawn breath expanded his massive chest, threatening the worn chambray shirt. His other hand enveloped hers, and he studied the blue-veined slenderness in his dark fingers.

"I know I'm ornery, and I say and do all the wrong things, little bit. But I'm not your father, and I'm not mean. And I know you shared something pretty special with your husband that I could never match."

He turned her wrists within his loose grasp, stroked the inner satiny texture with the rough pad of his thumb. "What I'm saying is it's a long, lonely life, honey. I care for you; it tears me apart to see you trying so hard to leave me. You must work fourteen hours a day between helping Mike with his college applications and painting lessons; then you paint and spend time with the kids and make the girls' new school clothes. Your nerves are stretched tighter than a rope on a calf. You're tired; that's the problem now."

The raw pain stretching out to her made Sami's stomach hurt. Ben's tenderness threatened the safety of the walls she'd built around herself; all the old pain of caring ripped through her once more. She slid her hands from his. "I'm not up to this right now, Ben," she murmured softly as she turned her head from his searching gaze.

"It's an old-fashioned idea, honey. But I want to take care of you. You're my woman and you always will be," he murmured raggedly. "Make up your mind. You're going to have a helluva time getting rid of me."

- 10 -

"THE TOWN OF Lone Pine has been having this little fair and rodeo every August since Ben first began the rodeo circuit," Banjo informed Sami as they sat on the board bleachers surrounding a dusty arena. "Tonight the Cattlemen's Annual Ball will be held at the Old Concord Hotel. Ben rented a suite there so we can change before the ball. Emma and Dan will take the girls home. I imagine Mike and Judy Thacker will go on the youngsters' hayride."

The hefty business manager pulled a strawberry-flavored tuft from his cotton candy, wadded it into a pink ball, and ate it. His red hair clashed with his fuchsia and green orchid shirt in the early afternoon sun. "I hear you weren't too happy about going to the ball."

"It was the manner in which I was asked," Sami answered. "Ben told me that if I didn't go, he didn't see any reason why he should either, and the Cattlemen's Association could find someone else to present the awards and dance the first dance with the mayor's wife."

Banjo chuckled. "You would have been in the local doghouse if Ben didn't show up tonight." He ate another tuft of cotton candy, then continued, "Ben was prepared to stay home all day if you didn't come to the rodeo, and that would really have made people mad. Ben holds classes on calf roping, bulldogging, and bull riding for the youngsters, then gets on top of the choicest sidewinder, horse or bull, to show them he still knows how it's done. All the proceeds go to charity. It's sort of a Wyoming cultural entertainment."

"Hi, good-looking." Eileen sat down next to Banjo, her jean-covered hips bumping his heavier ones to make space on the wooden bleacher. "Hi, Sami. I'm glad to see you. There's been plenty of gossip about you and Mr. Woden. Didn't I tell you the bigger they are, the harder they fall?"

Sami looked at her friend over the rims of her glasses. "There's usually not a whole lot of truth in gossip, Eileen."

"Humph!" Banjo interjected. "There is in *this* gossip."

Eileen's penciled eyebrows rose. "Really? You mean the boss man of Woden and Son Multicorporation and the star of today's rodeo is in love?" She eyed Sami's sleek chignon, pink cheeks, and rose-sprigged shirtwaist dress appraisingly.

"He's not the only one in love, from where I sit," Banjo murmured around another mouthful of cotton candy.

Sami glared at him. "You can just go sit somewhere else then, Mr. McGee."

"Can't. I promised Lori and Mary Jane they could bring all their friends over here and I'd explain the finer points of rodeoing to 'em. And I promised Ben I'd keep an eye out for you."

"Banjo, I am thirty-two years old. Have you ever heard of women's liberation?" Sami volleyed back.

"Ah, Sami . . . you're not going to cost me a good job, are you? Ben can get meaner than a wounded grizzly," the ex–rodeo clown coaxed. "Have a heart."

"Testing . . . one . . . two . . . three," the loudspeaker blared from the announcer's box. "Mr. Benjamin Woden, retired World Champion of the Rodeo Arena, will demonstrate his skills today, folks. All proceeds from today's activities will go to charity. Take your seats, ladies and gents. The Junior Barrel Racers will start the festivities, followed by Queenie Duvall, star of the bareback riders, performing on her horse, Pegasus."

Accompanied by a flurry of giggling girls, Lori and Mary Jane scrambled up on the bleachers. Lori grinned at Sami. "Gretchen and Linda are Judy Thacker's sisters. We met them when we went to see their kittens. Gretchen and Linda, this is our aunt Sami."

"It's nice to meet you." Sami smiled as the girls settled, balancing colas and munching on corn dogs swabbed with mustard.

The Junior Barrel Racers rode figure-eights around the appropriately placed barrels within the arena, their tall flags whipping against the clear sky. After their performance, Queenie Duvall, glittering in sequins, charged into the arena. Standing on Pegasus's back, Queenie somersaulted over the galloping horse, landing in a perfect handstand on his mottled rump.

When Queenie and Pegasus galloped out of the ring, the announcer led the audience's applause. "She's just as good as she was the day she won her title at the Omak Stampede in Washington State, folks. In fact, she's better. Now Ben Woden's son Mike will give a calf-roping demonstration. Mike is riding Ben's Appaloosa champion, Revenge; Mike will rope one of Elmer Johnson's heifers. Some of you old-timers may remember that Ben was just about Mike's age when he started out on the rodeo circuit. But we've just found out that Mike will only perform in the Lone Pine Rodeo; he's headed for college. Good luck, young Woden, hope you've got your piggin' string ready."

Dry-throated, Sami half listened to Banjo's explanation to the young girls clustered about him. "As soon as the gate is opened for the calf, Mike will run him down and lasso him. See that six-foot piggin' string hanging from Mike's mouth? As soon as he can wrassle that little dogie down, he'll do three wraps and a half hitch around the calf's back legs and one of its front legs."

"Is that the way the old cowboys did it, Banjo?" Lori asked.

"Yep. Watch. It's going to happen just like it did at branding time on the old Santa Fe trail."

The gate opened and the calf raced out, followed by Mike and Revenge lunging from the roping box. The roping occurred just as Banjo had predicted, and Mike received a standing ovation. "That was good time for roping a big calf, Mike. The timekeeper said you made nine and a half seconds. Congratulations!"

After another flurry of applause, the announcer spoke up again. "Now for the event you've all been waiting for . . . Performing only for us . . . World Champion Cowboy Ben Woden will ride Killer Blue. Killer is listed on the professional rodeo stock charts as the meanest Brahma bull on the circuit. An eight-second ride on Killer is a long, hard ride. Quiet now, folks. Let's not spook Killer."

"Oh, my God." Sami didn't realize the prayer had slipped over her lips until Banjo patted her shoulder clumsily.

"Killer's a sissy compared to the bulls Ben rode when he was on the circuit. Killer's a spinning bull, but Ben's only going to stay on him for eight seconds."

Numbed, Sami stared at the closed gate of the chute. A ton of blue-white monster rattled the sturdy hinges. Ben, dressed in a buckskin hat, a red-checked shirt, and leather chaps over his jeans, climbed to the top board of the chute.

From the distance, Sami saw the blaze of teeth in his tanned face. Her heart stopped.

"Oh, my God," she repeated, as Ben lowered himself carefully onto Killer Blue's back. He eased his leather glove through the loop of the thick rope circling the bull.

"She's going to faint. I knew it," Banjo muttered. "Ah, honey, he's not going to get hurt. He's in pretty good shape for an old man. This is the highlight of the whole day."

Trapped by her fear for Ben's life and limbs, Sami could not turn away from the sight unfolding before her. Her hand fluttered to cover her mouth, a gesture that would not still the feeling that her stomach was crawling slowly, surely upward.

The gate opened. Killer Blue charged out.

Ben's right hand gripped the loop; his left hand jerked off his hat and whipped the air. Incensed by the man's weight behind his quivering hump, the bull went into a series of bucking spins, lifting Ben's lean rear into the air.

The bull charged into the arena's fence, crashing against it. Killer Blue's rope caught on a board, then came free. Dust clouds followed the animal's spinning, tornadolike progress into the center of the arena. Ben's hat flew into the air. It landed in the dirt, and Killer stomped it as the cowboy began to slip sideways on the bull's back.

The announcer's concerned tone carried over the grandstands. "Oh-oh, folks. Bad news for the champion. Killer's rope was torn when it got caught on the fence. It's unraveling now. . ."

One furious buck broke the damaged rope. Ben was thrown free, flip-flopping in the air as Killer continued to buck. The bull's sharp hooves just missed Ben's head when he sprawled on the arena floor.

As though they were a single person, the audience stopped breathing. Unconscious, Ben lay on his back; maddened, Killer butted the arena boards a few yards from him.

In that dangerous instant, everything suddenly became clear in Sami's mind: She loved Ben Woden. She loved every rugged inch of him, every contrary turn of his personality. She was committed to that love—to that man—forever. And she had to tell him *now!*

"Damn!" Banjo cursed, following Sami as she jumped to her feet and crawled between the boards separating the arena from the crowd. She kicked off her heels as she ran to Ben.

Sinking to her knees beside him, she heard Ben's groan. The bull made roaring noises, and Banjo yelled, "Get the hell out of here, Sami!"

"Ben! Ben! I love you," she whispered, shaking his shoulders with all her strength.

Without opening his eyes, Ben groaned. "Hell, I know you do. I knew it the first time we made love . . . I love you, too, honey."

"Ben! Get off your lazy backside and get her out of here!" Banjo shouted, using his brightly colored shirt as a toreador's cape in front of Killer's beady eyes.

Not four yards from Ben and Sami, the Brahma bull pawed the dirt, undistracted by Banjo's flapping shirt and calls. The animal's huge head lowered in the direction of the fallen man and kneeling woman; his nostrils flared on either side of a steel ring.

Sami wasn't frightened. She was numb. She gaped at the bull, realizing the danger to herself for the first time. "We love each other," she said slowly.

Ben jackknifed to his feet, muttering, "You sure picked the wrong place to say all this, woman." He looped one arm around her waist and ran, half carrying her toward the fence. Banjo leaped in front of the bull, sashaying about the white-blue murderous mountain like a wildman.

Ben slipped Sami through the arena fence to safety, then followed her. Banjo, agile for his size, scrambled between the sturdy boards just fractions of a second before Killer's bulk crashed against the fence.

Wrapped in Ben's strong arms, Sami clung to him as though her life depended on it. They were safe now, but she shook, feeling both cold and hot at the same time. Ben's heart slammed against her as his arms tightened about her waist and raised her to his kiss.

Hot and primitive, his mouth locked to hers. Her hands framed his face, loved the thrusting bones beneath her palms, and splayed her fingers through the crisp waves at his temples.

His lips ravaged her tear-stained face, pressed against her ear roughly. In her arms, the length of his body shook, his breath ragged against her face.

"Oh, Ben . . ." He was alive. It didn't matter who watched; she didn't care. Her fingers roamed the hardness of his face and shoulders, reassuring herself that he was safe from harm.

When his head finally lifted, the gray eyes twinkled. "So you love me, huh? It took you long enough to find out."

Sami didn't want to talk. Shaking, she lodged her face in the safety of his neck and shoulder, uncaring as his left arm scooped up her dangling legs. He carried her into Queenie Duvall's dressing tent, announcing to the gathering crowd, "Show's over, folks. Leave my woman and me alone, okay?"

Ben closed the draped tent flap with a nudge of his shoulder. He sat down on Queenie's canvas cot, carefully holding Sami on his lap. He rocked her, crooning gently until she managed to halt her tears.

When she shuddered a final, deep sigh, Ben's leather-clad fingers tilted her chin up. "Here, blow," he instructed as he placed a handkerchief to her nose.

Sami obliged with one last shuddering sniff. Tenderly, he touched her lips with his, then asked softly, "You're not going to leave me now, are you, little bit?"

All the walls were down, and Sami knew her heart was in her eyes as she stared at the man she loved.

"Is Auntie all right, Benjamin?" The sound of Lori's timid voice caused Sami to turn toward the tent flap.

"Auntie is fine, Lori. You and Mary Jane can come in," Ben said as he eased Sami's head to his broad shoulder.

"Damn, we were scared spitless . . ." Mary Jane's reversion to her previous use of the King's English went unnoticed as Lori placed her arms about Sami, who managed a weak smile. For this moment, her nieces' vocabulary was not a priority.

She held them both. "I'm okay, pumpkins. Everything is just fine."

That night at the Cattlemen's Ball, dancing in a ballgown she'd borrowed from Rainey Johnson, and wrapped in Ben's arms, Sami knew she indeed loved the cowboy who was so different from Des.

She had confirmed it when she had left her bedroom in their suite at the Old Concord Hotel and Ben had risen from the overstuffed settee. Dressed in a western-cut black suit and white frilled shirt, he could have posed as a riverboat gambler. The glow from the chandelier lighted the crests of his dark brown waves, caught the silver sparks that glimmered there. The hard planes of his brow and jaw seemed to change, his smoke-colored eyes darkening when she entered the room. His stare locked with hers, and time spun out of control.

Slowly, inch by inch, his gaze trailed down the green satin mass of ruffles and the long hooped skirt. His grin was sensual, bearing all the impact of a bulldozer on Sami's emotions. Ben could be impossible, maddening. A gentle, considerate lover who razed her heart's walls.

He touched the pearl studs in her earlobes and held

out a small box. "Try these, pretty lady. I'd be proud if you'd wear them instead."

Now, as they danced, his strong arms enfolded her, and Sami felt as though she had stepped back through time into a previous century. She floated, guided by his practiced lead as they waltzed. His lips nuzzled her ear. "I'm glad you like the earrings, honey. I was afraid you might not take them."

"I love them, Ben. They're such a pure green, they look like emeralds."

His frown was puzzled as he pivoted her into series of swirls. "I wouldn't give you less than real stones, honey."

Sami's slippered feet seemed to lock to the polished tile floor, her hooped skirt billowing about his long legs. "Ben! If these are real emeralds, they're worth a fortune!"

His head went back; his scowl grew indignant. "Now, little bit, I know I pressured you into coming. But we're having a good time, aren't we? Or at least I am. I've got the prettiest woman in Wyoming in my arms, and every man here is envious. It's a pretty good feeling. Are you going to start tangling about a little pair of earrings?"

Before she could reply, his scowl darkened. "What the hell are you going to say about the damn ring, then?"

"Ben!"

"Damn! Come here, woman. I want to hold you."

The next day, Sami lay in the old hotel's bedroom suite and stared at the crystal chandelier glittering in the morning sun. She attributed the uneasy feeling swishing about in her stomach to the buttered lobster she had eaten at the Cattlemen's Banquet. The rich food and the very careful rein Ben Woden had kept on himself when he kissed her forehead at her bedroom door would have unraveled anyone's nerves.

"'Night, honey," he had purred in a tone that had made her want to lock her arms about his lean middle and drag him into her bed. "Think about me. Sleep tight."

She punched her pillow, crammed it beneath the curve of her neck, and scrutinized the flashing prisms dangling from the chandelier. Ben was all male devastation. When he wanted to, he could turn on the charm. The matrons of Lone Pine had really swooned as he twirled Sami around the ballroom floor. She punched the pillow once more. Ben Woden was one hunk of a white-toothed, dark-haired beautiful man. He was also the gentlest man she had ever known other than Des.

Des. She remembered him with love, but Ben's feverish lovemaking transported her into another world; he demanded everything from her and left little room for memories of another man.

"Hell!" Ben's curse prefaced his entry into her room as he tried to balance a wicker breakfast tray. Seeing him, Sami felt her heart go still. Dressed in yellow western-cut shirt, blue jeans, and polished boots, he didn't look as if he'd danced until three o'clock in the morning.

The pewter stare darkened as he turned to her and halted, tray in hand. "Good morning, pretty lady," he rasped in a tone that told her he wanted to join her beneath the satin coverlet. "I'm not used to balancing these damn things. I'll get used to it, though," he murmured half to himself.

"Are you going to marry me?" he continued in the same even tone. "We love each other, and the way I see it, if we don't tie the knot soon, you'll lose so much weight the wind will blow you away. And I'm not fond of sleepless nights and this ulcer I'm babying." He grinned. "Well, those are three good, practical reasons to get married. I think the first one is the most important—I love you, you love me."

Sami's nerveless fingertips tugged the coverlet higher about her bare shoulders. Ben walked toward her bed, concentrating on balancing the tray and placing it over her thighs.

He unrolled the red linen napkin, placed it beneath her chin, and lifted a long lock of satiny hair from her shoulder. "You've got that stricken look, Sami. Your eyes are big as saucers. Hungry?"

"Ben . . ." Everything he did was unexpected. Last night she had thought he'd take her in his arms; she hadn't expected the brotherly kiss at her bedroom door. He'd just asked her to marry him, and now he sat on the edge of her bed as though he were already a well-trained husband having a leisurely conversation with his wife before beginning the day.

Ben would never be a well-trained husband. He was too volatile. When he wanted something, he pounced.

He had that hunter's look in his expression now. "How are your applications for jobs going? Any really good prospects?"

Sami distrusted his sudden interest in a subject he had previously avoided. "I'm having problems getting the salary I need. I would have been in a better position if I'd started applying at the top of the year," she reluctantly admitted.

"I don't see any reason for you to go through all that," Ben stated bluntly. "We need an office manager for our company. You could do that easily."

Sami stared at him. Granted, she loved him. Perhaps she would marry the man, just to keep him out of trouble. But he had to learn a thing or two. "Ben, when are you going to stop moving things around to suit you? I'm a teacher. I enjoy my work, and I'm good at it."

His thick eyebrows shot upward. "Now, back off, little bit. Just because a man wants to take care of his woman—"

"Taking care of me doesn't mean smothering me, Ben Woden!"

The next morning, Ben left the ranch house grumbling that there were just too many people popping up at the wrong times. "What I want to do, woman, doesn't require an audience," he said, rising from the breakfast table.

"Ben!" Sami flushed wildly, unable to escape his searing kiss on her lips as Dan and Emma watched.

"I want some time alone with Sami," he had stated calmly, eyeing the older couple and his son.

"Why?" Lori and Mary Jane chorused.

He had tugged the girls' braids playfully. "Because she's so cuddly and sweet."

"It's okay with us if you cuddle her now. You did okay when you kissed her. She liked it," Mary Jane offered.

"Ben . . ." Sami warned, though she knew she wanted the same thing. She rather liked the possessive glide of his silvery eyes down her body. It raised tiny pinpoints of sensual expectation that she knew Ben could fulfill.

Later in the morning, Dan and Emma took the children for a picnic, and Mike went to Judy's.

Sami, aware that Ben truly wanted to be alone with her, could not keep her mind on anything but him. She settled for rearranging the living room furniture.

Bent over one edge of the large leather couch, pushing it in front of her, Sami didn't notice the opening and closing of the front screen door.

"Still moving things around to suit you, Sami?"

A chill ran through her as she recognized the down-home drawl. Sami spun around to face the large, leering man. "Jimmy!"

"That's right, honey child. You knew I'd be coming after my kids, didn't you?"

"You can't have them! You signed them over to me."

"Huh." As tall as Ben and as fit, Jimmy sauntered toward her confidently. "My, you're a whole sight prettier than your sister." The compliment soured Sami's stomach. This man had cared little for her ailing sister and less for his own children.

The light in Jimmy's blue eyes was greed. Sami recognized it clearly. "You're not taking those children anywhere. You signed away any right to Lori and Mary Jane. I have legal documents that state they're under my care." She'd fight him any day, anywhere, but he was not taking Lori and Mary Jane from her.

"A father's rights are big time now, sugar face. I've been reading how men are regaining custody of their children through the courts. I could just tell the judge that I was . . . grieved. Too wrapped up in misery to realize my children were being taken away from me by you and your hot-shot lawyer. Besides, I've remarried, and any judge will see that two parents are better than one. Especially with this Woden guy keeping you in his house."

"Jimmy, you're not fit to raise a toad; a judge has already said as much. You never took care of Lori and Mary Jane at all."

His eyes skimmed the room appraisingly. "This Woden guy has got a lot of money, I hear. The grave-monument people said his name was on the tab for your folks' and Ann's markers. He was easy to trace." Jimmy pivoted toward her. "I'm taking those kids back with me unless you up the ante."

"The custody fight took all the money I had, Jimmy." Sami began to shake. Jimmy had all the warmth of her own father. He knew little or nothing of love.

"Huh. Where are the scroungy little brats anyway? Get 'em or get me some money. Or I can hold 'em until you come across with the money. I want big bucks, Sami, not chicken feed." His avaricious eyes pried at

Sami's blouse and jeans. "Or maybe you can just work it off—"

Ben's drawl sounded at the front door. "I wouldn't touch her if I were you, Jimmy. I'm Ben Woden, and this is my ranch."

In a lithe motion, he pushed away from the door frame and walked over to stand beside Sami. The half lowered lids did not hide the dangerous glitter of his eyes as he smiled lazily down at her. "Hi, honey."

Sami saw the tension stiffen his muscled body as he turned to the other tall man. Jimmy's eyes darted at the cowboy, then down at her. "So that's the way it is," he breathed. "You ended up with a man this time instead of a spineless little bookworm."

"Have you got anything worthwhile to say before I throw you off my property?" Ben's chin jutted out, the cords of his neck hardening beneath the dark skin.

The situation was disastrous. Jimmy could be as mean as a cornered badger, but Sami wanted to deal with matters in her own fashion. Ben's lowered brows indicated he was not backing down; he was protecting her.

"I can handle this," she began.

"There's no 'handling' to it, Sami," Ben clipped out. "This excuse for a man is either going to clear out of your life or get his backside stomped."

Jimmy sneered. "A man comes to visit his own kids and he can't even see them."

"The court has made Sami, not you, their guardian." Ben glanced down at Sami. "Sorry, honey. But the girls brought me a legal document they'd found in one of your drawers. They wanted to know the meaning of a particular word."

He turned to Jimmy and said, "I had a fleet of top attorneys check those guardianship papers. The lawyer who drew them up knew his business. They're airtight, and the girls are legally Sami's."

"Ben . . ." Sami had fought for her independence all

her life. Jimmy just represented a rough place in the road; she could handle him—she'd done it before. She didn't want to hide behind Ben. "I can manage the situation."

"So can I." Ben's jaw ground from side to side, the fingers of one leather-gloved hand curled into a fist. Jimmy took a step backward. Chug growled, easing in front of Sami. Jimmy's eyes widened as he saw the bared fangs.

"Come ahead, big man," Ben dared Jimmy. "I'd really enjoy a go-round with you."

"Nah. It isn't worth it," the other man sneered as he skulked out the door.

Ben followed him with his eyes, then glanced down at Sami's furious face and crossed arms. He took a long, hard look at her. The thick black brows lifted then drew together in a frown. "What's wrong?"

Sami was frustrated, maddened by the way Ben had taken charge of a situation she could have managed with very little effort.

"You did it again. You just can't help yourself, can you?" she accused.

The thick brows shot up again. "What?"

Sami's finger wagged fractions of an inch from his broken nose. "Benjamin Wade Woden, I've been managing for quite some time without your assistance. I can stand on my own two feet."

"Honey. . ."

"Don't you honey me! So you had markers placed over my folks' graves? And Ann's? And you had lawyers examine my papers? My, you're a busy soul."

"I was going to tell you about the gravestones, little bit. When the time was right. Eileen told me how bad you felt about not being able to put up markers." He shrugged. "I thought . . . well, I thought it would make you happy, and that someday, after you saw them, we could replace them with stones of your choosing. But we haven't even had time to—"

"And who decides when the time is right, Ben Woden? You?" The flat of her hands hit his steel-hard chest once, then again for good measure. "You're always butting into my business."

"You said you loved me. The way I see it, that gives me rights."

Sami jammed her fists onto her hips. "I do love you. I just haven't figured out why yet."

"Propinquity? Your biological clock? The nesting urge?" he offered with an uncertain smile.

"No. Because you're a big, mean, ornery old pole-cat. And somebody's got to love you. It might as well be me."

- 11 -

SHOWERED, FRESHLY SHAVEN, and smelling of his best English cologne, Ben shifted Lori on his lap. He closed the storybook. "And they lived happily ever after."

Settled in his huge armchair, Ben looked over the head of the sleeping girl to Sami. She avoided his half-smile, ignored the flash of hopefulness in the thickly lashed, smoky eyes. Inside her simmered conflicting emotions: She loved him, but Ben had to stop treating her like a yard dog's tasty bone.

Curled into her corner on the couch, Mary Jane said sleepily, "I want my bed, Auntie."

Banjo ambled in from the kitchen. "What's that I hear? Somebody wants to go to bed?" He eased Lori from Ben and whispered to Mary Jane, "Come on, little dogie, let's hit the sleep trail and wait for Mr. Sandman. I'll tuck you in."

After a round of Mary Jane's kisses and Banjo's insinuating wink, they departed. Sami leafed through a current issue of a women's magazine. Ben had had that hunting aura all through dinner and into the early evening; he was too full of compliments, too good-looking, too . . .

From beneath her lashes, she glanced at his tall, rugged body. Eileen was right, she admitted. Ben Woden was the crème de la crème of masculine confections, whether dressed in his best suit or in his dusty jeans. Stealthily, she scanned his lounging physique from his expensive boots upward. Nice long legs, she decided, appropriately muscular beneath his new Levi's. He had a flat midsection that would never get paunchy, and a broad, broad chest and muscled shoulders.

She remembered the texture of the hard chest beneath his western-cut yellow shirt. Warm. Not too hairy. Just enough little black whorls to keep her playful fingers busy. And he had this cute little mole just south of his right nipple.

But it wasn't just Ben's physical attributes she loved. It was his compassion for other people, his sensitivity in dealing with the girls' problems, as well as his deep love for and pride in Mike.

Behind the protective shield of the magazine, she let her lips curve into a slight smile. Ben thought of her as his woman; his life-mate. To protect her from harm was instinctive—he had acted out of love this morning. She knew that deep in her bones, in her heart.

The fire crackled in the stone fireplace, warding off the chill of the mid-August evening.

Sami had just received an interesting reply to one of her letters of application: A school in Casper had an opening. Sami knew she should have called to arrange an immediate interview. But she was procrastinating. To be truthful, she couldn't stand the thought of leaving Ben.

He cleared his throat. "I like the way you arranged the furniture and hung your landscapes on the walls . . ."

She flipped two pages of the magazine. The sensual timbre of his deep voice reminded her of his high-handed ways. She was still raw from his handling of Jimmy. Who did Ben think babied her before he entered her life?

"The new drapes and these little tassled pillows are nice," he continued, adjusting a woven, cream-colored pillow behind his back. "Gives the place kind of a wifely touch."

He just kept coming. If he didn't treat her like yesterday's bulldogged steer, they could have an easier relationship. That was the problem, Sami decided as she flipped through three more pages of photographed casseroles. "Thank you," she murmured tightly.

Ben could spin cowboy tales that would fascinate the loftiest intellectual. Proud of his Wyoming roots, Ben was a source of its history and wildlife lore. If only he wouldn't pounce . . .

"Pink is a pretty color on you, Sami." The sensual, gravelly tone raised goose bumps on her bare arms. "Is that dress new?"

He didn't treat her like a bulldogged steer, she corrected. Every touch, every glance, proved he found her desirable and wanted her. Those tender nuances definitely excited and unnerved her. Even now, his compliment slid over her like a warm satin sheet. It wasn't in Ben Woden's character to make polite chitchat. She looked at him suspiciously over the rims of her glasses. He didn't need to know she hadn't been able to sleep and that she had made the pink shirtwaist instead. "Relatively."

"If I asked you to come over here and sit on my lap and tell me you love me, I don't suppose you would. Would you?" he pressed in a deep baritone that reached inside Sami's lower stomach and heated it.

She stared at him evenly and admitted to herself she badly wanted to do just that. "No."

"Standoffs call for drastic measures, honey," he threatened smoothly, then chuckled as she raised the magazine higher.

"How about a game of stud poker, Ben?" Banjo suggested as he descended the stairs.

At the midnight hour, the house was too quiet. Sami watched the aspen leaf shadows dance over her bedroom wall. She promised herself that she would have a serious talk with Ben in the morning.

She had to deal with reality. First of all, she would call the Casper high school and schedule an interview. If she got the job, she'd enroll Lori and Mary Jane in the Casper school system. Then she'd find a place to live. Her VW, still stored in Eileen's garage, needed to visit a good mechanic before it clattered down any highway.

Tomorrow, she decided, she would have a logical discussion with Ben. She needed space, and Ben had to allow her to make her own decisions. They were both intelligent adults. Their love just needed a little fine tuning, and, in time, they would adjust to each other's very different personalities. Ben could stop pacing the floor. She could sleep. It was a very sensible plan—to give themselves time to better understand each other.

She sighed and decided to count the leaf shadows until she finally drifted into sleep.

Some time later, she sensed movement in her room, felt the quilt wrap about her tightly before she was fully awake. The heavy fabric immobilized her struggling limbs.

"Shhh, little bit. There are just too many people around every time I try to get close to you, woman. I'm kidnapping you," Ben whispered huskily as his lips seared hers.

He wanted to see if he'd correctly read those shy little signals she'd sent him over the edge of her magazine. Once his tongue slid between her open lips, he felt her stop breathing. Her groan entered his mouth as she relaxed against him.

He moved quickly then, bundling her in his arms,

kissing her breathless as he went down the stairs two at a time. "Banjo's watching the girls," he whispered as he opened the door. He kissed her hard again, closing the door with his boot heel.

"Ben, I'll scream," Sami threatened as he seated her, blanket and all, on Revenge's saddled back. He swung up behind her. "You can't just . . .

He nuzzled the tender place at the base of her neck, nibbling the silken, fragrant skin. "I apologize, sweetheart. But desperate men do desperate things. Especially old men in love."

"Huh! You don't sound sorry, and you don't act very old. I doubt that Mike would try this trick," Sami sniffed just before his fingers eased back her long hair and his parted lips trailed down the curved perimeter of her ear.

"Mike's on his own." His teeth tugged her earlobe. "Good, you're not wearing those damn little spiky things," he noted with satisfaction. "I wonder how many men have choked to death on them." When she stopped breathing, he asked, "What's wrong? Cold?"

"Oh, why should I be? You just hauled me out of a warm bed. You know very well what's wrong. You're a distracting man."

"Yep. But you're the first woman I've ever tried *all* my charms on," he murmured. "I'll get better at it as time goes by."

He loved the way she snuggled back against him even as she sighed, "You're hopeless."

"Yep." He turned to the Saint Bernard loping beside Revenge. "Go home, Chug. I can handle this."

He felt himself begin to harden. The denim across his hips was suddenly too tight as Sami's nose nuzzled the hair on his chest. "I planned to have a serious talk with you in the morning." Her lips moved restlessly against his flesh, heating it.

The smooth warmth of her cheek brushed his open collar and settled at the base of his neck. The slight caress, the pliancy of her small but enticing body beneath the heavy quilt promised Ben something he'd fight to keep. Sami had to realize she belonged with him. Anywhere she chose. Hell, it didn't matter where; he'd traveled all over the world. Lord, he needed to see those big brown eyes darken to velvet black as he made love to her.

He grinned, resting his chin on top of Sami's fragrant head, imagining her long black hair spread across him in a gigantic satin-sheeted bed. Maybe in Paris. They could tour the Left Bank and the Louvre. He could buy her frilly little nighties and scanty panties. His grin widened.

Standing wrapped in her quilt, Sami watched Ben unroll his sleeping bag. He had stashed it on the little knoll where they had first made love. He had also hidden a portable inflater and an air mattress. He arranged the oversized sleeping bag on the inflated mattress. She shook her head. Life with Ben would never be dull.

In a patch of moonlight beneath the pine boughs, he lodged Mike's portable radio–tape deck against a rock and inserted a cassette. Humming off-key to the sound of Mancini's orchestration, Ben unwrapped two long-stemmed crystal glasses. He placed them carefully on a napkin spread over pine needles and propped a silver thermos against a pine-tree trunk. He stripped off his jacket, rolled it into a mock pillow, and placed it at the top of the sleeping bag.

The Rocky Mountain chill seeped into her, and the downy warmth of the sleeping bag looked inviting. Sami shivered within the folds of the quilt.

"Cold?" Ben's teeth flashed in the moonlight as he stood and faced her. "Come here, honey. I'll warm you up."

His voice shattered the last of her resolutions. She knew that her master plan for time to adjust wouldn't hold up to the sensual onslaught his tone promised her. Rough and deep, his voice skimmed warmly down her body. It seeped into her hips, covered by her sensible white panties, and down the length of her thighs. It locked into her knees, weakening them, then seemed to slant the rocky ground beneath her bare feet.

Ben was done hunting. He had come to collect his woman. Sami read it in his long-legged stance, in the tilt of his head. She was proud of the fact that he wanted her desperately, that he needed her warmth in his life. She knew she would leave the knoll committed to the tall rancher. But she was determined not to make it easy for him. After all, she, too, had pride. She caught her bottom lip between her teeth and worried it.

"Now, little bit," he rumbled confidently over the sound of violins. "I guess I'll just have to come over there and get you."

Sami intended to enjoy her capitulation. She vowed to make Ben's romantic rendezvous on the moonlit knoll something he would dream of when he was ninety. He'd crashed through her vow not to love again. Now he'd have to suffer the consequences of his action.

She moistened the fullness of her bottom lip with the tip of her tongue, and Ben's lazy, sensual expression sharpened to one of hunger. She lowered her lashes to peer at him through the black spikes.

Huskily, she tried her best Mae West imitation. "You'll just have to come and get me, big boy."

Ben's eyes were shadowed, but his heavy eyebrows jammed together. "Sami?" he questioned uncertainly.

She loved it! He deserved a little of his own for constantly throwing her off-balance.

Sami tilted her head, and the mountain breeze wrapped a wispy lock of hair across the planes of her cheek. She allowed the quilt to slide off one bare white shoulder.

Ben's low indrawn breath was a ragged contrast to the smoothness of the romantic music. "Damn. What have you got on under that thing, woman?"

He took the two steps between them in one stride.

Sami fluttered her lashes, staring up at him as she once more moistened her lips. "Almost nothing, darling."

Ben's hand rose slowly. A fraction of an inch from her cheek, it stopped. His warmth touched her flesh before his large palm rested gently on the contours of her jaw. It trembled slightly as the rough pad of his thumb caressed the sensitive corner of her mouth. Sami parted her lips slightly, turned, and sucked his thumb into the heat of her mouth.

The full moon outlined his bent head in a silvery glow. His other hand drifted to wrap about her neck, his thumb sliding down the long, slender length of her throat.

Minute electric charges shot between them as Ben stared down at her upturned face. Slowly, both big hands cupped her face, and he smiled tenderly. "You're going to make me pay, aren't you, little one?"

Sami merely smiled.

One of Ben's thick brows arced upward. "I had this all planned, you know, right down to seducing you with a shaker of Fuzzy Navels and a platter of Emma's best Cheddar cheese sticks."

"And then?" Sami allowed the quilt to ease down her other shoulder, aware of the quickening of Ben's warm breath as it brushed her face. He swallowed, staring hungrily at the darkened crevice between her breasts.

Ben's voice drifted off. ". . . make you see reason . . . put my ring on your finger." The last words escaped on a husky whisper. "I thought I could . . ."

"Oh, you can, Mr. Woden." Sami leaned forward fractionally and nuzzled his broad chest. Her lips parted. She breathed moist, tantalizing circles on the whorls of crisp hair.

A heavy shudder rippled through Ben. His breath stopped when Sami tugged open his pearl shirt snaps with her teeth.

She skimmed his moist skin with the tip of her tongue, found a nipple and circled it. Ben groaned. She trailed tiny kisses across the muscled width of his chest until her teeth nibbled on the other hardened tip.

"Sami, stop it," he protested weakly. "I was going to tell you about all my plans to reform. Hell, I didn't even try to arrange a teaching job for you at Lone Pine in the new program for gifted children that just got funding in time to begin this fall. When Ray asked if you'd be interested, I told him he'd better talk to you."

"I'm proud of you, darling." Sami let the quilt fall to her feet, studying Ben's reaction to her almost nude body.

His gaze followed the sloping curve of her chest, touched the uptilted tips of her breasts. Ben swallowed slowly, his eyes drifting lower to her brief-covered hips and slender thighs. "You're a beautiful woman, Sami."

"You make me feel beautiful, Ben," she corrected huskily. The hunger gnawing in her lower stomach matched the melting, golden heat flooding her upper legs. She fitted her palms over his bare midriff, smoothed the dark skin lightly. Delicately, she trailed one finger downward, following the tapering black chest hair. She toyed lightly in his navel, and Ben's stomach jerked inward as he gasped.

Sami slid her left hand upward, gliding over the thick, corded length of his throat. "I can't reach your mouth from down here, cowboy," she hinted.

Ben seemed to have regained his balance. "Here, honey. Let me help you," he offered, sliding his palms down her sides to her waist. He pressed the small indentation, then eased his fingers beneath the elastic waistband of her panties. He cupped her derriere, lifting, sliding her upward until her face was on a level with his.

Sami's arms locked about his neck. She rubbed her nipples against him. She touched his lips with her tongue and drew open-mouthed circles on his lips. A woman could enjoy exploring a man like Ben Woden for a lifetime.

Ben's lips plagued the softness of hers. He nibbled at

her flushed face, stroked her softer cheeks with the shaven smoothness of his jaw. Against her temple, he asked, "Aren't you cold?"

"I'm getting warmer, cowboy," she managed as he raised her higher. Trailing open-mouthed kisses down the length of her throat, Ben pressed his face into the valley between her breasts. He nuzzled the firm globes, teasing them until his mouth closed over the nub of her left nipple.

Sami skidded into passionate hunger. Her hand cradled the back of his head, urging him to take the fullness of her breast deeper into the moistness of his hot mouth. A gentleman catering to his lady's needs, Ben obliged.

"Oh, my..." Sami arched, pressed her hips more fully against the thrust of his jean-covered hips.

"Easy, honey," he whispered roughly, lowering her to stand on the downy sleeping bag. Easing her between the flannel folds, Ben gently tucked the edge of the bag beneath her chin. He stood, legs spread.

Arms akimbo, Ben stared down at her. Despite her hunger, Sami reveled in the fact that she was his woman and he was her man. It was an elemental fact, not debatable.

Desire flowed in the shadowy hollows of his eyes and cheeks, firmed the dark flesh stretched over his brow and prominent jaw. But a tenderness roamed there, too. Sami knew it was only for her.

Ben's expression was one of pleasure. His gaze roamed over her long hair as it framed the white oval of her face and spread across his folded jacket.

"You're a pretty picture, woman. Big brown eyes all soft and waiting. Lips sweet as honey and looking like crushed petals. Any man would love to have you in his bed every night."

"You're not too bad a sight, either, Benjamin," she countered softly, remembering Ben at the Cattlemen's

Ball, looking like a riverboat gambler, skillfully waltzing her until three o'clock in the morning.

"I love you, Samantha."

"I love you, Benjamin."

He began to undress. His shirt fluttered down to cover the pine needles. Sami hungrily followed the lithe, muscular form outlined in the moonlight as he pulled off his boots and socks. "Are you going to marry me?" he asked, unbuckling his brass champion belt.

Of course she would. Heart thudding against her chest, Sami challenged the man she loved. "Are you going to eat broccoli and cheese quiches and listen to Bach?"

"Yep. I'm a changed man, honey. No more drinking. No more fighting. And no more bull riding. I can't afford to have you run into the ring with a ton of bull pawing the dirt. You've given me too many gray hairs already." He unzipped his jeans and slid them down the muscular length of his legs.

Ben grinned slowly as Sami stared at his hard body. "Some things never change, woman," he teased. "Move over."

When Ben at last held her, his heart thudding heavily beneath her cheek, Sami knew her lonely search was over. This was home.

He stroked her upper arm lazily. They enjoyed the pleasure of lying together in the sleeping bag. Sami trailed her fingertip across his brows and down the broken line of his nose.

"Nice."

"Mmmm," he agreed. "This bag is a close fit. I think I'll have one custom made for us before we go camping up in the Rockies. We can let one of the kids use this one." He rubbed his hairy thigh over Sami's smooth, slender one, easing the palm of one hand over her breasts. He massaged the soft weight, then drew concentric circles on the hardening tips.

Sami shivered. "Where are my Fuzzy Navels and cheese sticks?"

Ben shifted her, wedged her tightly against him as his arm crossed her back and his hand smoothed the jut of her hip. He lifted her chin. "Are you going to marry me?" he asked urgently. "Or am I going to follow you for the rest of our lives?"

Sami's soft palm feathered across the hard muscles of his chest. She nestled against him, smiling.

She toyed with his nipple. "I'll think about it."

"Maybe this will help you make up your mind," he growled, easing her beneath him, stripping her panties from her.

Propping his weight on his forearms, Ben held her face. "I would have liked a little more room in the sleeping bag tonight."

"Excuses, excuses. You'll just have to make do," she taunted lightly.

Ben's grin was slow, masculinely confident. "It'll be a first. I seem to have a lot of them with you."

She smoothed his ribs with her palms in feather-light motions, allowing them to drift to the hollow of his back, then curve about his lean buttocks.

She smiled at his indrawn gasp. "Watch it woman. I've got a lot of things to say before you jump the gun."

Sami's small hand edged upward. Around his hips and between them. She held him. "What gun, my love?"

"Sami . . ." Ben shuddered even as his hips began to move against the caress of her fingers.

With the ease of a small woman guiding a big man, Sami shifted, juxtaposing Ben's desire with hers. She rose as his muscle-corded arm slid beneath her, nestling her aching breasts to the hard planes of Ben's broad chest.

She caressed him more firmly, easing her thighs from beneath the weight of his heavier ones. Breathing harshly, Ben lay in the cradle of her upper legs. She stroked the backs of his knees with the soles of her feet and watched his hunger grow. "The promises can come later, Ben. Don't make me wait," she whispered against his descending lips.

Ben's lips promised. Hungrily, his tongue plunged into the warm, moist sheath of her mouth, dueled with her own. It trailed over the sharp edges of her teeth until Sami sucked it rhythmically, holding it in her mouth.

Her right palm feathered his muscle-ridged back, felt his skin ripple beneath the skimming caress. She flattened her hand between his shoulderblades as she anchored her legs to his.

Ben's face nuzzled the tender area behind her ear. "Sami, my dearling, my lady love," he murmured as he pressed her deeper into the air mattress.

His hair was cool on her chest as he slid down, fitting the furnace of his mouth over her left nipple. He took great care, laving the aureola with his tongue, massaging the velvety weight with his fingers until he elicited her groan.

Sami's fingers tightened on his desire, urging it into the fragrant nest of curls at the joining of her thighs. Instinctively, she slid the hardened tip against the slick, moist heat.

When Ben's mouth slid to her other breast, framed its aching perimeter with tantalizing kisses, Sami's skin flamed. His teeth teased her nipple, tugging the hardened bud. Her body tightened as the pleasure mounted to a sensual ache deep within her, her hips lifting against the hardness of his, searching . . . urging . . .

Ben continued to tease her breasts, though she tasted the salt of sweat on his shoulder, nipping it. Opening his mouth wider, Ben suckled deeply and Sami went wild, twisting higher, urging him deeper.

"Oh, my . . ." she moaned, her head thrashing from side to side as she felt him withhold the ultimate fullness from her aching core.

With a jerk, Ben unzipped the sleeping bag and slid

lower down Sami's soft, vibrating body. He tongued her navel, and Sami felt her lower body begin to tremble, the moistness there increasing to match her passion. Massaging her breasts, Ben blazed a heated trail across the soft planes of her stomach.

When he nuzzled the fragrant curls, Sami gasped. "Ben! I need you. I love you."

"Hmmm?" Intent on seeking pleasure and giving it, Ben continued stroking her body. He seemed to enjoy the molten flow of her beneath his hands. He touched her reverently, as though she were priceless, a delicate work of art.

But Sami needed to be treated like Ben Woden's woman. She slid both hands into his hair to tug him higher on her body. Before Ben settled fully upon her, his fingers slid into the moist, fragrant mound. Skillfully, he produced vibrating contractions as he watched Sami's eyes darken. Shaking, embracing him with all her strength, Sami yielded to the hot, rippling tides washing over her, minute explosions charging through her veins. She gasped. "Ben . . ."

Helplessly, she arched against the pressure of his hand. "Ben . . ."

Urgently, Ben's long fingers touched her sensitized flesh until a sunburst of colors burst behind Sami's closed eyelids. She sank weakly into a velvety warm cloud.

When her eyes opened slowly to Ben's tender smile, she sighed, drained.

He touched her lips lightly with his own. "Are you going to marry me?"

"Yes." The wisp of a word was too great an effort.

"Then I'd better get serious . . ." He eased over her.

"Ben, I can't . . ." But when the full, hard length of him slid inside Sami, she found that she could. When his tempting kisses changed to a hot, urgent hunger, his thrust quickening within her, Sami met his passion and matched it with the fire of her own.

- 12 -

"COMFORTABLE DOWN THERE, Sami Soon-to-be-Woden?" Ben drawled a long time later that evening. Sated from their passion, he balanced a plastic container of homemade cheese sticks on his lean stomach. He sipped a Fuzzy Navel from a long-stemmed crystal goblet and cuddled Sami closer to him.

Wrapped snugly in the crook of Ben's strong arm, Sami placed her empty goblet on the pine needles beside them. She nuzzled his still slightly moist chest with her nose, skimming his familiar male geography with her palms. "Tonight's setup is perfect, right down to the air mattress. You're a resourceful man, Mr. Ben Woden."

"Mmm. I've always thought so. Not every man can wrangle with the Wyoming Wildwoman and come out a winner. Put another cheese stick in my mouth, woman."

Sami obliged, giggling. "Feeling ten feet tall, master?"

"Feeling very satisfied, Wildwoman. You made an old man of me in just a few minutes."

Sami giggled again. Because that was how she felt inside. Happy. "You'll recover, I'm sure."

"Uh-huh. I'm just taking a breather."

Pine cones crunched as large, dark shapes slid by Ben's makeshift pallet, gliding through the firs and pines. "Deer coming down from the mountains for the winter," Ben explained. "Revenge would be acting up if it were mountain lion or bear."

A coyote howled on another knoll. Staring at the twinkling stars, the lovers listened to the mournful loneliness. After a while, Sami asked, "What did you say about Ray's offer before—"

"Before we got serious?" He grinned down at her, lazily palming her breast.

Sami flushed. Ben had meant business. He had taken her to wild, heavenly heights, pacing his own pleasure to hers.

He set aside his empty goblet and the plastic dish. "Oh, no, honey. I'm not mixing in your career decisions, but I'll act as a sounding board if you have difficulty making up your mind."

She raised herself up slightly, loving his broad grin in the moonlight. Ben Woden was a totally appealing man. She decided to test his resolve. "I got a nice offer from a school in Casper. They need a special education teacher."

Ben frowned, thinking. But he didn't hesitate. "It's up to you. It's your career, honey. As a matter of fact, I looked at a nice little piece of property not far from Casper. I could run a few cattle and my business, too. Dan and Emma have managed this place for years. I could give it to them in lieu of the retirement pensions I'd planned."

"You're a caring man, Ben. But I think I'll talk to Ray. I'd like to live here. I like the Lone Pine School."

"Uh-huh." He stroked the smoothness of her upper arm beneath the sleeping bag. "I know I'm pushing, and we'd have to run it through a lawyer, but what do you think about me adopting Lori and Mary Jane after we're married?"

He tilted her face up with the tip of his finger when she hesitated. "Oh, Ben . . ."

"Oh, now, little bit," he groaned. "I can't stand to see you cry. I turn to jelly." He kissed her eyelids. "Don't worry about it, honey. But the kids call me Daddy every once in a while, and it will only confuse them to have a different last name than our own kids. I thought it might be a good idea . . ."

"I'm crying because I'm happy, darling," Sami sniffed.

"Well . . . don't cry. The sight of it jerks me inside out. You're all I need, anyway. Here . . ." He reached into his jeans pocket, rummaged through it, and extracted a small box. "I picked this out a long time ago. But if you don't like it, we'll go shopping for another one. Maybe when we take our honeymoon in Paris—"

Sami stared at the rectangular-cut emerald Ben placed on her finger. "Ben, it's huge!"

"Damn right. But I plan to buy you some Parisian panties that are barely scraps." He felt for her sensible cotton undies with his toes, reached down to hook them with his hand. The white ball sailed into the closest stand of sumac sprouts.

"Paris?" Sami echoed. "Paris, Texas, or Paris, France?"

"This is important, Sami," he growled. His look of utter disappointment melted Sami's resistance. She fluttered her lashes at him, deciding that flirting with Ben was a sport she'd like to explore to the hilt. She stroked her palm downward, feathered his flat stomach, and was rewarded with his rough gasp.

"Now, Ben, honey." She kissed the base of his throat, loving the way his pulse slammed against her lips. "Do you realize that I haven't seen you in the altogether? In the light?"

"We can fix that problem later, honey. But you're not going to see another man like that," Ben warned.

Sami nuzzled his chest. He smelled like all man. Brushing the tip of her nose through the still slightly damp whorls of his chest hair, she cuddled nearer the rangy length of the cowboy she loved.

"Men are different," she mused, skimming her hands over his hairy thighs. "Furry."

She finger-walked down Ben's left thigh. It quivered, and his arms tightened around her. "Sami," he said sharply, "I'm not done talking yet. And you're distracting me plenty." He swallowed. "I want you to know that I'll pass that damned GED test whenever you think I'm ready. I talked to Mike, and he said it wasn't hard. We can't have you married to an uneducated lout, can we?"

"Uh-uh," Sami murmured, examining the lobe of his ear. She nibbled it as he had done to hers.

He shivered. "Sami!"

She lifted her face to his, kissed the intriguing mold of his lips. "Now, Ben. Be fair. We're going to be partners, right?"

"Hell, yes. But I was going to save the really difficult maneuvers until we had a king-sized bed beneath us. You're moving a little too quickly, honey."

She Eskimo-kissed his nose with hers. "Ben, honey. I'm ready now."

Ben's thick eyelashes closed as she once more skimmed her palm down his hard, waiting body. "Let me be your lover, Sami," he murmured huskily. "Let me be your friend."

"Always, my love."

With a kiss beneath the Wyoming stars, the cowboy and the schoolmarm sealed their pact to share a lifetime together.